BEQUEST TO A TEXAN

From the day of their arrival, the Texans realized it would all happen again. Hart City had more corrupt officials than was good for the law-abiding, over-taxed citizenry. But the late Ed Gelbart had left them a list of notable locals — those they could trust; those who they must oppose, the conspirators preying on the community. When the tall men went into action, all hell broke loose in the big town.

MARSHALL GROVER

BEQUEST TO A TEXAN

A Larry & Stretch Western

Complete and Unabridged

LINFORD
Leicester

First published in Australia in 1990 by
Horwitz Grahame Pty Limited
Australia

First Linford Edition
published 1996
by arrangement with
Horwitz Publications Pty Limited
Australia

British Library CIP Data

Grover, Marshall
　　Larry & Stretch: bequest to a Texan.
　　—Large print ed.—
　　Linford western library
　　1. Australian fiction—20th century
　　I. Title
　　823 [F]

　　ISBN 0–7089–7914–9

Published by
F. A. Thorpe (Publishing) Ltd.
Anstey, Leicestershire

Set by Words & Graphics Ltd.
Anstey, Leicestershire
Printed and bound in Great Britain by
T. J. Press (Padstow) Ltd., Padstow, Cornwall

This book is printed on acid-free paper

1

The Last Adios

"**B**IGGEST funeral in the history of Hart County," declared Joe Mirram, editor of the local newspaper. "Well, it'd have to be, right Doc?"

"What we'd expect, yes," agreed Lewis Richmond, M.D., gazing across the crowded cemetery. "The county's wealthiest citizen. So many people, hundreds of them. Small wonder we can't get any closer to the graveside."

The thin-faced newspaperman patted the note book tucked under his arm and remarked,

"Quite a eulogy Deacon Petrie delivered. I'm glad he's no fast talker. I got it all."

"You'll print it," guessed the aging medico.

"Page Two, next edition," nodded Mirram. "Appropriate, don't you think? Deacon said all the right words and, when a cattle baron dies, it's not just big news. It's part of the Arizona Territory's history."

Other locals of note were no closer to the next-of-kin at the graveside than Mirram and Doc Richmond. During the singing of the last hymn, the greying, angry-eyed Dave Trant, a well-to-do merchant of the county seat, nudged his companion, covertly indicated four men standing together and said softly, but bitterly, "Damn hypocrites."

"No harsh words, Dave," chided Abner Doble, founder and manager of Hart City's only independent bank. "This isn't the time."

"Come on, Ab, you share my suspicions," muttered Trant.

"You know I do," said the banker. "But we're helpless. Suspicion without proof is — well — just that. Suspicion."

There must have been few hired

hands on duty at Lone Star, the biggest cattle outfit in the county, probably in the whole Arizona Territory. As well as the immediate family and the house servants, the leathery foreman, Duff Wheatley, had mustered no less than thirty-two riders to escort the two surreys to the cemetery this afternoon.

It was generally assumed the foreman was of an age with his late employer. If that were so, he was wearing well and showing no indications of the heart disease that had claimed Edward Jesse Gelbart. Even in his going-to-meeting town suit, Duff Wheatley was every inch the veteran, durable cattleman, a tall, weather-beaten man, greying but straight-backed, and, like his old friend and boss, Texas-born. Had Doc Richmond ever been obliged to medically examine the ramrod of Lone Star, he would have found little if any excess fat.

When the grave was filled in, tradition was observed; people queued up to express their condolences to the

3

remaining Gelbarts, the matronly Elva Gelbart Sherwood, first-born of the late Edward and Sadie, her portly husband, Morton Sherwood, six foot Jesse Gelbart and his delicate wife, Trudy, and the younger brother Vernon, as handsome as Jesse, but two years younger and an inch shorter.

When lawyer Gordon Crouse, executor of the deceased's estate, took his turn to confront the family, the imperious Elva cut short his expressions of sympathy.

"Kindly wait by the Lone Star vehicles, Mister Crouse." It was a command, not a request. "We'll expect to find you there no matter how many more people feel obliged to speak to us."

"We have questions," said Elva's husband, eyeing Crouse sternly.

"At your service, Mister and Mrs Sherwood," nodded Crouse, and moved on to where the short and slender blonde was flanked by her husband and brother-in-law. He identified himself, adding, "We met briefly three years ago, gentlemen, under equally sad circumstances, the funeral of your mother."

"Yes, I remember you, Mister Crouse," said Jesse. Five years his sister's junior, he was dark-haired and handsome, his keen eyes as blue as his wife's. "I thought then, and still do, that my father's legal affairs were being handled by a very young lawyer."

"Appearances can be deceptive," Crouse said self-consciously. "My next birthday will be my thirty-ninth."

Trudy Gelbart paid him a compliment, but briefly, as this was a solemn occasion.

"That is a surprise, Mister Crouse. I'd have assumed you to be twenty-five at most."

"I hope I'm as fortunate at your age, sir," said Vernon Gelbart. The youngest of the Gelbart offspring was also the most ebullient, always good-humored; though mourning his father's passing, he almost grinned at the lawyer. "Quite an achievement."

5

"Kind of you to say so," Crouse acknowledged.

He left them to make his way through the crowd to the line of vehicles in the street below the cemetery entrance. There were surreys, buggies, buckboards, jumpseat wagons, every kind of rig. Once clear of the crowd, he surveyed all he could see of Hart City. The county seat was big and impressive. He had never been as far south as Tucson, two hundred and fifty miles southeast as the crow flies, but visualized it as a dusty place, a scattering of adobe structures not to be compared to the handsome buildings bordering Hart City's wide and busy main street.

He stood by a vehicle wearing the emblem of the Gelbart cattle empire and waited patiently, anticipating Elva's questions and reflecting that, like it or not, she would just have to accept his answers; he would honor his late client's every instruction. And surely that was the least he owed the cattle baron he had so admired.

After several dozen more locals had offered their sympathy to the family, Jesse quietly enquired of his brother, "Getting weary of all this?"

"Not at all," was the reply. "People respected the old man, Jesse. And, despite our contrasting temperaments and ambitions, so did I. He earned all these tributes."

"Well, Vern," said Jesse, "That's something we'll never argue about."

"Don't draw any wrong conclusions, Trudy," muttered Vern, linking arms with his fragile sister-in-law. "Your man and I never argued about anything that I can recall. We were never rival siblings."

"You're so different, you and Jesse," she murmured.

"In every imaginable way," nodded Jesse. "But what Vern says is true. Good to be able to say that at this time, right Vern? We always got along."

"That could be a tribute to your

forbearance, big brother," opined Vern. "You were the steady one. I was the day-dreamer with the wild notions."

"Our parents didn't hold it against you," recalled Jesse. "I guess I just followed their example." He dropped his gaze to his wife's pallid face. "Not weakening, are you, honey? People will understand if I take you back to the surrey. Maybe you should be off your feet?"

"I'm managing," she said.

Another quarter-hour passed before the next-of-kin were able to leave the cemetery. They here followed by the Mexican family Bedoya, Mateo, Carmen and their daughters Rosa and Juanita, their late father's house-servants, and Duff Wheatley and the Lone Star hands.

The spread's blacksmith climbed to the driver's seat of the first surrey. Crouse, standing beside it hat in hand, was now addressed by the Sherwoods.

"This delay — about the reading of the will — is most inconvenient,

Mister Crouse," complained Elva. "We are anxious to return to Sacramento. Our children have been left in care of their governess, our housekeeper and the room maids."

"And I can't neglect my business interests," declared her husband. "Confound it, man, I own and run two of the biggest hotels in Sacramento."

"I've already explained . . . " began Crouse.

"No need to fret about the kids, Sis," interjected Vern. "A governess, a housekeeper and — how many maids?"

"I resent having to entrust the welfare of our children to our hired help," snapped Elva. "And, Vernon, I hate being called Sis — as you're well aware."

"I stand rebuffed," shrugged Vern. "A thousand pardons, dear sister."

"Mort, I'm sure the staff of the Californian and Sacramento Realto Hotels can function efficiently during your absence," soothed Jesse.

"It's not the same," grumbled Mort.

"If I may repeat . . . " Crouse tried again.

"It's intolerable!" protested Elva.

"As your late father's lawyer and executor, I'm duty bound to obey his instructions to the letter," said Crouse. "The will cannot be read till another beneficiary gets here. You already have my assurance every effort is being made to contact him. Unfortunately, he's somewhat nomadic, so it may take a little time."

"That's all we know about this other person — all you'll tell us about him," she said accusingly. "Just that he's hard to locate. You won't even name him."

"I'm not at liberty to do so until he arrives, until I escort him to the ranch," said Crouse. "Please believe, Mrs Sherwood, I do regret the inconvenience. However . . . "

"Now, see here . . . " blustered Mort.

"However," Crouse persisted, "you must also believe I've no intention of

10

betraying the trust placed in me by your father."

"Excuse me," frowned Vern. "One point confuses me, Mister Crouse. If you cannot divulge this fellow's identity, how can you hope to find him?"

"I had no choice but to request the help of another party, Mister Gelbart," explained Crouse. "He'll be discreet, I assure you, and he's the man most likely to discover the whereabouts of this other beneficiary — because of the nature of his profession."

"I guess you mean the sheriff," Jesse concluded.

"Not Sheriff Apley," said Crouse. "A far more reliable source of information. Now, I crave your indulgence, but you must understand I can say no more than that."

"I'm sure you're doing your best," said Vern.

"And I see nothing to be gained by our bothering Mister Crouse any further at this time, Elva," said Jesse.

11

"By your leave, ladies," said Crouse, turning to leave them.

The Sherwoods began the journey north out of Hart City in the first surrey. Their driver, Lone Star's blacksmith, gnawed on half of a Long Nine and looked to the team, paying no attention to the disgruntled couple from Sacramento. Jesse, his wife and brother travelled in the second surrey. Their driver was the laconic Duff. The heavy escort party of cowhands kept their mounts clear of the vehicles. Bringing up the rear was the jump seat rig, the Bedoyas up front, their daughters in back.

"Never thought of the old man as being secretive," Vern remarked "He was a shrewd one, God rest his soul, a touch whimsical too."

"But never an eccentric," said Jesse.

"Never," Vern warmly agreed. "Much as I abhor fisticuffs — in my profession, one's looks are so important — I'd feel a compulsion to strike out at anybody who called him an eccentric."

"This business about the will, our having to wait for an unknown beneficiary, I can't begin to guess Dad's reason," frowned Jesse. "But we oughtn't forget he had a reason for every move he ever made never acted rashly, always had a purpose in mind."

"I'm glad neither of you resent it, as Elva does," said Trudy. "She's so upset, and I'm sorry about that."

"Jesse and I tend to be philosophical," grinned Vern. "When it comes to extreme indignation and high dudgeon — well — sister Elva is the specialist of the family."

After another mile, Jesse expressed his gratitude that, upon being advised of their father's demise, his children had been able to come to Hart City in time for the funeral.

"Not too difficult for us, Vern, getting here from San Francisco, and Elva and Mort travelling from Sacramento, but yours was the longest journey."

"Chicago," remarked Trudy. "More

than a thousand miles away."

"I didn't get around to asking," said Jesse. "Were you working or, as you actors say, at liberty? Did you have to quit a show?"

"I'd have done so, naturally, had it been necessary," said Vern. "As it happened, the drama in which I was playing second lead closed the day before I received the lawyer's telegram. My thanks to the railroad and stage-lines. I wish I could have made it earlier. Arriving this morning was cutting it fine, but at least I was in time for the funeral."

"You must be near exhausted," said Trudy.

"Haven't even had time to unpack." Vern nodded and stifled a yawn. "I think I'll sleep till suppertime."

"My brother the actor," Jesse commented with a wry grin. "So how's show business?"

"Thriving," said Vern. "I'm becoming known and working with some of the top professionals. Too bad the old man was taken aback by my theatrical ambitions, but I like to think it was some consolation to him that I'm doing well. How about you? He was just as surprised that you scorned the cattle business in favor of becoming an accountant. You're consolidating your position with the Cullen and Drew combine I hope?"

"Jesse is in charge of the accounts department now," Trudy said proudly.

"Congratulations, big brother," offered Vern.

"Thanks," said Jesse. "Dad knew about my work, knew C and D is a meat packing and export outfit. Maybe that pleased him — my having *some* connection with the cattle business."

To his sister-in-law, Vern gently remarked, "I was saddened by Jesse's letter concerning your illness. A great disappointment for you both, I'm sure, but I won't distress you with a long speech Trudy. I'll just wish you a speedy recovery."

"Thank you, Vern," she acknowledged.

"Speaking of sleep . . . " began Jesse.

"Yes, I'll rest this afternoon, I promise," she nodded.

Gordon Crouse's business address was an office above a photography parlor on South Main Street accessible by a narrow flight of stairs which the editor of the Hart County *Journal* climbed in haste at 4.45 that afternoon.

Mirram was glad to find the lawyer alone. He entered wearing an encouraging grin and Crouse at once took heart.

"A clue to his whereabouts?" he asked eagerly, as the newspaperman helped himself to a chair.

"Good information," declared Mirram. "The Gelbart heirs should not be kept waiting much longer. Promised you I'd put out feelers, didn't I? The old reliable grapevine of the Fourth Estate, Gordy,"

"What have you heard?" demanded Crouse.

"Just got a wire from a friend, editor of the Gibb County paper," announced Mirram. "Gibbsville's only a two-day ride east of here, as you already know."

"And . . . ?"

"And Valentine's there, Valentine and his partner. What's more, there's little danger of their riding out of Gibbsville rightaway. I'd say late tomorrow at the earliest. So draft Valentine a wire and I'll take it along to the telegraph office for you. You need only send it care of the Gibb County sheriff . . . "

A load had been lifted from the lawyer's shoulders. No more heavy badgering from the bumptious Mrs Sherwood. He could now assure her the will would be read to the family in the near future. He was profoundly grateful to Mirram and said as much.

"I owe you a big favour, Joe."

"Don't give me too much credit," said Mirram. "Chalk it up to coincidence. We just got lucky."

"I assume Valentine and Emerson are in custody at Gibbsville?"

17

"Any of us would assume that, but no, not this time. They're being delayed in Gibbsville by a trial. My colleague used the word 'prolonged' and informed me those trouble-shooters are prosecution witnesses."

Crouse's pencil was busy.

"Legal proceedings sometimes end abruptly," he fretted. "So I'd be obliged — since you've offered . . . "

"Keep your hopes up," urged Mirram. He rose as the lawyer proffered the message. "I get this away right now, the Gibbsville sheriff should be receiving it before nightfall." He started for the door, then paused. "You still can't tell me why old Ed wanted Valentine here?"

"Privileged information, Joe, and I rely on you to maintain secrecy till after the will is read," Crouse said firmly.

"And then?" prodded Mirram.

"And then," said Crouse, "the terms of the Gelbart will become an open secret."

Gibbsville was the seat of another cattle community of the Arizona high country, the verdant terrain a good distance west of the Painted Desert end many a long mile from the arid land around Yuma and Tucson. Though not as sizeable as Hart City, it did boast a courthouse.

And its sheriff was the barrel-chested Patrick O'Dowd, who received the wire from the Hart City lawyer while at supper in a Chinese restaurant a half-block from the county jail. Forking up mouthfuls of chow mein and munching pensively, O'Dowd squinted at the Western Union envelope and conceded he should not open it, should keep the lid on his curiosity. There was his name sure enough, a name of which any Irishman should be proud, but with a c/o preceding it and the other name above it — L. Valentine.

"So it's for you, Mister Famous Trouble-shooter," he mused. "But in

19

my pocket it will stay till tomorrow morning. Maybe that locked-up jury'll reach a verdict tonight, but I'll not bet my badge on it, the way that blabbermouth lawyer from Phoenix operates."

Larry Valentine, like his long-time compadre Stretch Emerson, was a restless spirit, O'Dowd well knew. What was the substance of this wire from Hart City? He couldn't even hazard a guess, but he figured he understood those nomadic outlaw-fighters and their impulsive ways. Find them, deliver the wire rightaway? No sires. Better tomorrow morning, when they would be firmly anchored right where prosecution witnesses belongs their backsides in seats in the courthouse. If Valentine were to read this message tonight, he might well pull a fast disappearing trick, head hell for leather out of Gibb County with his partner, and their absence would be noted by the already irritated and irascible Circuit Judge Ellery Purnell.

True, The Texas Trouble-Shooters had not yet irritated Judge Purnell. As chief witnesses for the prosecution, they had done their duty with surprising dignity and shown the judge his due of respect; no complaints, no reprimands from the bench. The cause of all Purnell's irritation was the hot shot, high-priced, long-winded lawyer brought to Gibbsville from the territorial capital by the well-heeled father of one of the defendants. Long-winded was putting it mild, O'Dowd reflected. Mr Raymond Fry was a lawyer in love — with his own rhetoric. A compulsive orator and straw-splitter obviously bent on securing an acquittal for his client despite all the damning evidence.

What if the jury couldn't reach a verdict? Wouldn't it be just like that gabby Fry to make yet another speech doing his utmost to discredit Messrs Valentine and Emerson? And what if Messrs Valentine and Emerson just weren't present?

"Holy Saint Patrick — old fire-eating Ellery might blame *me*," O'Dowd warned himself.

That settled it as far as he was concerned. He would hand the telegram to Larry Valentine, but not tonight.

9.15 of the following morning, the courthouse again crowded, bushy-browed Judge Purnell fixed his rheumy eyes on the jury foreman and asked, "Has the jury reached a verdict?" The foreman got to his feet. "Yes sir, Judge."

Purnell raised his eyes to the courthouse's fly-specked ceiling and fervently declared, "Thank You, Lord. And you know I mean it."

He ordered the foreman to announce the verdict. "We find the defendant, Lucas Tohler, guilty as charged."

The defendant, a lank-haired twenty-three-year-old whose right arm was in a sling, promptly rose and called the Jury foreman an obscene name. So did his wealthy father, probably resenting the high fee he would have to pay the defence attorney as much as he resented the jurys verdict. Purnell used his gavel to quell the uproar, fined Tohler Senior $100 for contempt of court, then glared balefully at the dapper and pomaded lawyer from Phoenix.

"Before passing sentence, I have something to say about the conduct of the defence in this case," he declared.

"Everybody stay quiet now," O'Dowd rose just long enough to voice this order. "Just hush up and listen."

"I'm obliged, Sheriff O'Dowd," nodded Purnell. "Obliged to you, to the county prosecutor and the witnesses, but not to you — Mister Raymond Fry from Phoenix." His eyes gleamed. "This was — or *should* have been — what is often referred to as an open and shut case. The chief prosecution witnesses, Valentine and Emerson, actually fought and apprehended the defendant in the act of holding up a southbound stagecoach — Lucas Tohler and his accomplices — and delivered all four of them to the county jail. Their testimony, supported by that of the stage crew and passengers, was conclusive, Mister Fry!"

Without rising, Fry smoothly reminded him, "Every accused man is entitled to as thorough a defence as can be provided. That's the law, Your Honor."

"Damn it, counsellor, do you suggest a veteran circuit judge should brush up on due process of law?" scowled Purnell.

"I was merely pointing out . . . " began Fry.

"You were about to launch another speech, confound you," growled Purnell. "Probably as lengthy, as high-blown as all the oratory you've subjected us to since this trial began. Well, by Godfrey, it's too late. The prisoner has been found guilty, the verdict's in and now I'm doing a little summing up, now it's *my* turn to orate. But, unlike you, I'll express myself succinctly."

"If it please Your Honor," shrugged Fry.

"But for your delaying tactics, this

case could have been settled, over and done with in one day," complained Purnell. "It has lasted *four* days! You are certainly within your rights in giving the accused the best defence you could manage, but did you have to be so dratted long-winded about it?" He raised a hand. "That question requires no answer. I have only this last comment to make before I pass sentence. It is my sincere hope — indeed I'll *pray* — that it'll never be my misfortune to preside at another trial with Mister Raymond Fry performing as defence counsel!"

"I accept your rebuke," smiled Fry.

Purnell glowered at the prisoner, who glowered right back at him, and passed sentence.

"Lucas Tohler, you having been found guilty of armed robbery, you will suffer the same penalty imposed on your accomplices. I sentence you to ten years imprisonment in the San Jose Territorial Penitentiary. Sheriff O'Dowd, take charge of the prisoner." He banged his gavel. "Court's adjourned."

The chief prosecution witnesses got to their feet as the courtroom began emptying, trading bored glances.

"Sure took long enough," grouched Woodville 'S' Emerson.

"Longer'n it ought to have," agreed Larry Valentine. "Just like the judge said."

"Makes damn near three weeks we been stuck in this town," Stretch calculated.

He was stating — accurately — that this was an aggravatingly long period for a couple of inveterate drifters to spend in any one place. The wander-urge of these uncommonly tall Texans was much a part of the legend of the lone Star Trouble-Shooters as their altruism and their instinctive hostility toward the lawless.

On their feet and falling in behind the people making for the courthouse entrance, their height was impressive. Larry of the dark hair and square-jawed handsomeness was of powerful physique and all of six feet three inches bootless. Stretch, that gangling, tow-haired, homely beanpole, topped his partner by a full three inches, which made him a six-and-a-half-footer. He was easygoing by nature, never a deep thinker unless necessity demanded, more inclined to leave all the heavy figuring to his more mentally agile partner; they had been partners, fellow warriors as close as brothers, for longer than they cared to remember.

They retrieved their sidearms from the rack beside the doorway and moved out into the morning sunlight. O'Dowd's deputies were returning the prisoner to the county jail. He stood watching them strap on their hardware, two seemingly ageless tumbleweeds in well-worn range clothes. Being ambidextrous with pistols, the taller Texan packed twice as much Colt as his companero; his matched .45s were housed in holsters slung from a buscadero-style shellbelt. They thonged their holsters down, and then the sheriff confronted them.

"For you," he said, presenting the telegram to Larry. "Came for you yesterday."

Larry squinted at it, also at O'Dowd.

"Yesterday?" he challenged.

"Round suppertime," nodded O'Dowd.

"Well, hell, you could've let me have it right-away," chided Larry. "You and your deputies knew where to find us."

"Bleaker's Hotel, Patrick," Stretch reminded him.

"Trial wasn't over, so I couldn't take a chance you'd up and skedaddle," said O'Dowd. "Wasn't forgetting you stayed on under protest. Well, boys, this was one of those times your affidavits wouldn't do it. With Cass Tohler bringing in that hot shot all the way from Phoenix to defend his lowdown son, the county prosecutor needed for you to testify in court."

He ambled away.

"The saloons're open and I'm thirsty," said Stretch.

"I need a long cold beer as much as

you do," Larry assured him.

"Wouldn't believe you if you said you didn't," was Stretch's rejoinder. "C'mon, let's irrigate."

They sauntered to the nearest saloon and, in a matter of moments, were breasting a bar, hooking bootheels on the brass rail and half-emptying tankards. Larry then tore the flap of the Western Union envelope, extracted the telegram and read it.

"Sonofagun," he frowned.

"Who's it from?" asked Stretch. "Doc Beaumont in trouble? Our old buddy Slow Wolf maybe?"

"We never heard of this hombre," muttered Larry, rereading the wire. "G D Crouse it's signed, attorney at law."

"We don't need a lawyer," protested Stretch.

"Seems *he* needs *me*." Larry was still perplexed. "Imperative, it says here."

"What's that mean?" wondered Stretch.

"Extra important, kind of," shrugged

Larry. "Imperative I proceed to Hart City and parley with him."

Next question," shrugged Stretch. "Where the hell's Hart City?"

The barkeep overheard.

"West of here," he offered. "On the railroad route. Big cattle town."

"Gracias," nodded Larry. "We won't be waitin' for no train. How long d'you figure it'd take us to ride there?"

"Couple days, maybe a mite longer," said the barkeep.

They finished their beers. Stretch shrugged again and remarked, "We got nothin' better to do."

"Uh huh," grunted Larry. "And I guess lawyer Crouse needs me for somethin', but I'm damned if I can savvy what." As they made for the batwings he reflected, "Might be Doc Beaumont had to shoot some tinhorn that cheated him and Mister Crouse is gonna defend him."

"We could be witnesses again?" Stretch winced, exasperated again. "Aw, hell. I've had my bellyful of courts."

"If it's Doc — or Slow Wolf — we'll likely be what they call character witnesses, somethin' like that," opined Larry.

"How's our bankroll?" prodded Stretch.

"Healthy," said Larry. "Five hundred, give or take a dollar. we'll buy us enough grub to last a couple days, then check on the fastest route to Hart City."

While a storekeeper was attending them, Hart City was mentioned; he had been there.

"Whole lot bigger than Gibbsville, fine town," he told them. "Mighty rich cattle spread in Hart County, the Gelbart outfit. Folks say it's the biggest in all of Arizona."

Larry paid for their purchases which were stowed in a gunnysack. From the store, they walked to the sheriff's office to find the boss-lawman relaxing at his desk. O'Dowd responded to their request by rising and leading them to the map on the wall right of the

31

jailhouse entrance.

"You could make it in two days," he calculated. "But the barkeep should've said northwest." He prodded at the map and they followed his moving finger. "Here's where we are now. You ride the northwest trail out of town till you come to a fork. Head straight north from there and, around this time tomorrow, you'll cross the railroad tracks and find a regular trail. It runs level with the railroad. You can ride it straight west all the way to Hart City." He added, in a not exactly unkind way, "I'll be glad to see the last of you, and you know why."

"We know why," agreed Stretch. "The longer we hang around any one place, the better our chances of gettin' in trouble."

"And that'd grieve me, boys," declared O'Dowd. "Texans you are, but it's well known there's more than a drop of good Irish blood in your veins."

"You suppose Patrick's got some Irish in him, runt?" asked Stretch.

32

"Ain't sure," said Larry. "O'Dowd? Irish name maybe. But it could be French or Dutch or . . . "

"Away with you," chuckled O'Dowd.

The tall men stopped by the Western Union office. Larry's wire to the Hart City lawyer was a masterpiece of brevity — 'On my way.' They checked out of the hotel, hefted their gear to the livery stable accommodating their horses, saddled up and rode out.

Larry's curiosity wouldn't let up. And Stretch? Though an optimist, he had come to what seemed an accurate conclusion, taking into account other occasions on which they'd answered a summons. That conclusion. They would find some kind of crisis situation at their destination.

Didn't they always?

33

2

He's On His Way

SINCE transmission of the all-important message to Gibbsville, Gordon Crouse had spent much of his time haunting Hart City's Western Union office, much to the bemusement of the genial telegrapher, Chester Harris.

Less than an hour after the Texans rode out of Gibbsville, Larry's reply was received; Crouse was on hand at that moment.

"This what you've been waiting for, Mister Crouse?" Harris asked, handing him the three-word message.

The lawyer took it, looked at it and nodded gratefully.

"Yes, this is it. Thanks, Chester."

"Guess I don't have to tell you," remarked Harris. "That L. Valentine

34

who sent it is mighty well-known. Been called notorious, come to think of it."

"I'm familiar with his reputation, his and his friend's," nodded Crouse.

"You, me and hundreds of people, maybe thousands," said Harris.

"I'd be obliged if you'd say nothing of this," pleaded Crouse, pocketing the telegram.

"Western Union respects the confidence and privacy of . . . " began Harris.

"Sorry," Crouse apologised. "I shouldn't have asked."

"Well," shrugged Harris. "It's one of the rules."

"For many reasons, it's important that Mister Valentine's coming to Hart County be kept secret, at least until he arrives," explained Crouse. "I'm afraid I'm a little nervous at present. You'll have to excuse . . . "

"It's okay, you don't owe me any beg pardons," Harris assured him.

On his way downtown to his office, Crouse was trying to decide the speediest means of getting word to kin of the late Ed Gelbart, his impatient daughter in particular. He was loath to travel out to the ranch at this time. Pay some local to deliver the good news? He could do that of course, but now he spotted a familiar wagon stalled in front of the Trant Emporium.

It was smaller than the rig used by Lone Star's chuck-boss when he came to town to purchase provisions for the spread's sizeable crew. This was the vehicle assigned to Mateo Bedoya who, armed with a list made by his plump spouse, was responsible for picking up supplies needed for keeping the ranchhouse kitchen well-stocked, the family supply wagon. Problem solved, he was thinking, as he quickened his step to speak to the Mexican now emerged from the store, a sack of flour balanced on a shoulder.

Mateo Bedoya was swarthy, as durable as Duff Wheatley and of genial disposition. He greeted the lawyer respectfully.

"If you're returning to the ranch as

soon as you've loaded provisions . . . "

"Si, Señor Crouse. Soon. No more than a quarter-hour."

"Please come to my office before you leave, Mateo. I'll give you a note for the Señora Sherwood."

"Ah si, the Señora Elva."

Crouse hurried on to his office. While composing a note announcing the impending arrival of another beneficiary, it occurred to him he could as easily address it to one of the Gelbart brothers. He was tempted to do so, but decided on diplomacy. Elva Gelbart Sherwood was the first-born, probably considered herself head of the family now — and there was also the fact that he resented her imperious demeanor and had no wish to clash with her. There *would* be a clash, he reflected. Hell, yes, a humdinger. Until he performed his duty and read the will, however, he would spare himself the aggravation; after all, his wife was expecting their third child.

He sealed the note, wrote 'Mrs

M. R. Sherwood' on the envelope and smoked his pipe until Mateo Bedoya knocked and entered.

"Here you are, Mateo. For the Señora Sherwood as soon as you get back to the ranch. And thank you."

"De nada, señor."

Soon afterward, the supply wagon was rolling north out of Hart City and the younger of Sheriff Apley's deputies entering the Trant store. Ritchie Neville wasn't as weighty as Apley's other aide. He was well-groomed with a lovingly-tended mustache, his manner brisk. As well as serving as a deputy sheriff, he was the administration's official tax collector. This latter duty winning him no friends in the town's business community.

Dave Trant finished serving another customer. When the woman departed, Neville smiled at him and stepped up to the counter; Trant had never liked that smile.

"'Morning, Mister Trant."

"It's not that day of the month,"

Trant said curtly.

"No, it's not," Neville acknowledged, still smiling. "I just came by to inform you the council has voted a ten per cent increase in property tax starting next month."

"Another rise?" scowled Trant. "This is news to me, Deputy, and I'm a councilman."

"Sure, but majority rules, you know?" shrugged Neville. "The mayor held a meeting over breakfast with the treasurer, and Councilmen Orban and Markey — must've forgotten to invite you and Councilman Doble. They voted unanimously so, if Holly Orban and George Markey agreed with the decision, I'm sure you and Abner Doble'll go along with it."

"Don't have much choice, do we?" frowned Trant.

"All in a good cause," drawled Neville, helping himself to a cigar from the open box on the counter. "Hart City folks know their tax money's handled carefully and used for the common good. That's efficient administration, Mister Trant. Everybody benefits. We have a fine city hall and courthouse, the best county school you'd find anywhere in the territory and soon we'll have a public library and a new theatre. These improvements're good for business. Think of all the people who'll come flocking here to see performances by famous theatre folks. Edwin Booth for instance, Lily Langtry, Eddie Foy and others of their kind."

"I can hardly wait," Trant said dryly.

"Visitors'd be paying for more than a theatre ticket," said Neville. "They'd patronize the saloons and stores, stay overnight in our hotels. It's all new money, you see? Like I heard Sheriff Apley say, everybody'll turn a handy profit, one way or another." He turned to leave. "See you tax day, Mister Trant."

"Deputy Neville," said Trant, when he was halfway to the entrance. The lawman turned, eyebrows raised. "Five cents."

"What?" said Neville.

"For the cigar," said Trant.

Neville chuckled, fished out a coin and tossed it. Trant caught it and watched him walk out. His wife then entered from the rear, asking, "What was that all about?"

"Another tax rise, Cassie," muttered Trant. "Ten per cent."

She grimaced.

"Are people taxed as high in Phoenix, Flagstaff, Tucson — I wonder?"

"Something will have to be done eventually," he declared.

"How far ahead is eventually?" she demanded. "And *what* can be done?"

"Has to be another election next year," he reminded her. "If we can put up a candidate to oppose Burford, maybe we'll have a new administration. Feeling's running high, Cassie. All it'd take would be for Burford's challenger to make tax-reduction his campaign."

"Till then, we can only live in hope," she sighed. Upon his return to lone Star, Mateo sought Elva before unloading the wagon. She was climbing the staircase when he came through the main entrance to-the great ranch-house.

"Señora Elva," He hurried to the stairs, moving up to her and doffing his sombrero. "For you, a message from Señor Crouse, the abogado."

She accepted the envelope, eyeing him coldly.

"Mateo, when you deliver a note, it should be on a platter," she chided.

'Muy triste,' he reflected, watching her resume her ascent. 'Once you were a muchacha altanero. Now you are a mujer altanero.'

In the upstairs parlor, Morton Sherwood was listening to his younger brother-in-law and waxing caustic, sceptical of Vern's dissertation on the future of the American theatre.

"Drama has come into its own, comedy also," the young actor declared. "Of course there are the musicals. They're generally referred to as musical comedy though, in truth, there's little humor in them. Great appeal for the growing emigrant element of the big cities, the Europeans. They may improve. That remains to be seen. But fine drama is my forte, Mort. Better playwrights are much to the fore now, brilliant dramatists, some of them . . . "

"Show business is just a form of amusement," insisted Mort. "What will make this country great is big business, commerce, industrial progress. The theatre is a minor factor," He looked up as his wife entered. She seated herself to read the note from the lawyer. "Has anything been heard of this — what should I call him?"

"The mysterious beneficiary," grinned Vern.

"At last some progress," frowned Elva. "Mister Crouse has received word that this person, whoever he is, should arrive soon. His idea of soon is within another three days." She tossed the note aside. "The waiting is so exasperating."

"That's all Mister Crouse has to say?" asked her brother.

"He'll bring the person here as soon as possible after he reaches the county seat," she said irascibly.

"Then we don't have much longer to wait," he remarked.

"The sooner this business is over and done with, the better for all concerned," grouched Mort. "We all have commitments. We're just hanging around here, and I share Elva's irritation."

"Dear sister, do you feel nothing for the old place?" challenged Vern. He gazed wistfully about the handsomely appointed room. "The home of our childhood. I've missed it. Chicago is where I live and work, but I'm relishing my time here. So many good memories. Don't *you* feel that way?"

"Why should I?" she demanded. "Sacramento is my home now, our children, Mort's business, our social ties, our friends."

"Too bad," Vern commented. "For

44

as long as we're obliged to stay on for the reading of Dad's will, we should be relaxing and remembering our earlier years. I believe that would make both our parents happy."

"I consider this Crouse fellow is being unnecessarily close-mouthed about the whole situation," complained Mort. "Why shouldn't he tell us who he is, this anonymous beneficiary?"

"We have a right to know," said Elva.

"We'll know, Sis, all in good time," shrugged Vern.

"Don't call me Sis," she retorted.

"Give Mister Crouse credit," appealed Vern. "Dad imposed certain conditions for whatever his reasons. As his lawyer and executor of his estate, he's abiding by those conditions, honouring all the old man's wishes. Just doing his duty after all."

"I can't imagine who the person could be," said Elva.

"You don't recall some old crony of your father's?" prodded Mort.

"When I settled in Sacramento with you, I was glad to forget Lone Star," she said. "I maintained a respectful and amiable relationship with my parents, corresponded regularly, but thrust all thought of other people from my mind."

In the upstairs bedroom they shared, Jesse Gelbart smoked his first cigar of the day and stared to the open window. Trudy was out there, standing by the balcony rail, studying the terrain far beyond the ranch buildings, the rolling green range across which the Lone Star herds moved and grazed.

She was taking deep breaths when he moved out to join her, inhaling, exhaling, smiling too.

"The air," she enthused: "So clear, so fresh."

I've rarely heard you cough since we got here," he remarked, wrapping an arm about her shoulders. "So we can believe the specialist, right? he said spending time in this part of Arizona could only be beneficial.

And something else, honey. You aren't so pale now. There's color in your cheeks."

"I'm starting to feel really well again," she declared.

"Great relief for both of us, his diagnosis," he said fervently. "Not tuberculosis, just a bronchial condition — curable in a better atmosphere."

"This is the better atmosphere," she assured him. "Much, much better, dear."

"Too much fog in our part of San Francisco," he muttered. "The state of your health — after your operation . . . "

"My resistance was low," she nodded.

"So the coughing began," he sighed. "That damn fog, a threat to your . . . "

"Stop worrying about it," she begged.

He moved away from her and lowered himself to a chair to finish his cigar. She stayed by the rail, the morning breeze caressing her. They were silent a while, sharing the same memory.

In the seventh month of their marriage, she had been rushed to hospital. A miscarriage — with complications. She had survived vital surgery; they could never become parents, but he was resigned to that, still giving thanks she was regaining her health. If only she would rid her mind of the foolish notion she had let him down.

She said it again now.

"Jesse, I'm so sorry."

"You're forcing me to repeat myself," he said gently. "Last time, sweetheart — please? No reason, *never* a reason for you to feel guilty, It's all right for you to experience regrets once in a while, but the good Lord knows you don't owe me nor anybody else an apology. It's just something that happens in some marriages. You're in no way to blame — you must realise that. And now we must pick up the pieces."

She turned to face him, nodding agreement.

"Yes, you're making good sense — as you always do. Very well. No more

48

brooding, I promise." With a half smile, she added, "I also promise to ignore Elva's uncharitable attitude. She doesn't put it into words, but the inference is always there, isn't it? She has given her husband three beautiful children and obviously considers I've failed you."

"My sister can be a pain in the butt," he growled, stubbing out his cigar.

Trudy couldn't suppress a chuckle.

"Such language, darling. But it matches your new attire." She was noting he had donned Levis and a rough work shirt; a bandanna instead of a cravat. "You look . . . "

"Not *new* attire," he grinned. "The kind of rig Vern and I wore in our boyhood and youth. We were raised here on the ranch, don't forget. A rancher's sons, not town kids. And, while I'm here, I'll find these duds more serviceable than a custom-made suit." He heard a knocking at the bedroom door and raised his voice. "It's unlocked."

49

His brother let himself in, crossed the room and came out to join them. Trudy was seating herself. Vern perched on the balcony rail and announced, "Only a few more days to wait."

"The lawyer's heard something?" prodded Jesse. "Mister Crouse is pleased to inform us, per medium of our impatient sister, that he's received a wire from the party concerned," said Vern. "Gave Mateo a note for Elva while our unofficial uncle was in town for supplies. She and Mort are still grumbling. Not my idea of cheery company, so I volunteered to apprise you of the latest development."

"This means Mister Anonymous is on his way?" asked Jesse.

"And our lawyer friend will fetch him out here as soon as he shows up, or as soon as possible thereafter," nodded Vern. Now he appraised Trudy. "Little sister-in-law, unless my eyes deceive me, your condition is improving."

"It is," she smiled. "We've just been discussing it."

"She's feeling a whole lot better, Vern," said Jesse.

"I'm glad," Vern said warmly. "When it came to claiming a site and sinking roots, Dad was no fool, big brother. This must be the greenest part of the Arizona Territory. Think what it would have meant to Trudy."

"If what?" frowned Jesse.

"If he'd founded this ranch far to the south," said Vern. "South of Phoenix, for instance, down around Tucson. Think of the high temperatures, all that alkali dust, a real threat to a young lady needing to recover from acute bronchitis."

"Mighty true, boy," said Jesse. "Take our word for it, honey. We've been down there, so we know."

"That bad?" she asked.

"Alkali is as fine as talcum," said Vern, grimacing.

"Penetrates everything — you're never rid of it," said Jesse. "Count on this, Trudy. If, for any reason, I have to travel down there again, I'll not take you with me."

"Your word is law, lord and master," she good humoredly replied. "I'm sure I'd hate dust as much as I . . . " She shook her head. "Never mind."

"Go ahead, say it," Jesse invited. She shook her head again, so he told his brother, and bluntly, "Fog. A lot of it in our part of the west coast."

"Yes, of course." Vern nodded thoughtfully. "Doc Richmond in town would probably — is he still . . . ?"

"Still in practice," said Jesse. "He was at the funeral, but there were so many people, you couldn't have spotted him."

"He'd probably blame exposure to damp and foggy conditions for Trudy's illness," opined Vern. "Trudy, you have just cause for hating it."

"Frankly, I'm not looking forward to our return to San Francisco," she murmured.

"Must you go back?" Vern asked

his brother. "You should give that question some thought, big brother. We can assume we'll inherit Lone Star, a third share each. I'll be going back to Chicago, but why shouldn't you stay on and take Dad's place? With Duff as active as ever and you in charge, the ranch would continue to function. I'd be in favor of that arrangement, and why should Elva argue about it? Of course, the big question is would you be willing to resign as boss of the C and D's accounts department?"

"Oh, Jesse . . . " began Trudy.

"All right, sure," said Jesse. "It's an idea, and worth thinking about, but we'd best postpone further discussion of it till after the will reading."

* * *

Later this morning, in the mayor's office at City Hall, Otto Kimmer was remarking, "He'll be a great loss to the community, old Ed, no disputing that. On the other hand, it's lucky for us he resigned from the council when he did."

The County Treasurer was of slight physique, a balding, sharp-featured man. By contrast, Mayor Moss Burford was burly and a shade under six feet tall, more assertive than Kimmer and more particular about appearances. He owned the Hotel, the biggest in Hart City, and was never as soberly garbed as Kimmer; his clothes were custom-tailored.

"Fine man, Ed Gelbart," he mused. "I was genuinely sorry when he vacated his chair as a councilman, but he had good reason you know. The pressure of running his cattle empire."

"The point is, he wasn't one of us," frowned Kimmer. "And we need to be just as wary of Trant and Doble. Especially Doble. He's a banker after all, a money-man."

"They're satisfied the administration's running smoothly," shrugged Burford. "What they don't know can't hurt us. And they provide a necessary balance,

Otto. The taxpayers might become leery of us, what with Holly and George on the council. Balance, my friend. The town's leading merchant and the only independent banker give us a touch of class."

"You don't think Trant or Doble are getting suspicious?" challenged Kimmer.

"I doubt it," Burford said confidently. "They're no threat and neither is Mirram."

"Even so, I'm thankful Mirram isn't a member," muttered Kimmer.

"And never likely to be," grinned Burford. "Meanwhile, he can't publish what he doesn't know and, even if he did know, he wouldn't have the nerve. Not all newspapermen are heroes, Otto."

"This tax increase — there'll be a lot of ill feeling," fretted Kimmer.

It's the human condition, a tradition," chuckled Burford. "Nobody likes paying taxes. Nobody ever has. Nobody ever will. But, when an administration decides they have to pay more, they go right ahead and pay it."

"Five months from now, there'll be another election," Kimmer warned.

"And I'll mount an even bigger campaign than last time," said Burford. "People enjoy my speeches, Otto. I tell them what they want to hear, I reassure them, remind them of how this town has progressed under the present administration. By the time I'm through campaigning, I'll have them believing they'd be facing disaster if they didn't re-elect me and my loyal aldermen. You take care of the accounts, my friend. Leave all other decisions to me."

★ ★ ★

Toward noon two days later, following the trail paralleling the railroad route to Hart City, the Texans slowed their pace. A grade dead ahead. If a westbound train could climb it, so could Larry's sorrel and his partner's pinto, but they weren't about to overwork their mounts.

"Somewheres up top, we'd best find us a place we can make a fire and cook us some chow," Stretch said raising his eyes to the heights. "It's that time, runt. My belly's growlin'."

"Might be we'll get where we're headed tonight," opined Larry.

"Can't be too soon for you, huh?" challenged the taller Texan. "You never could abide a mystery. So, from back when you read lawyer Crouse's telegram message, that busy brain of yours has been just buzz' with questions."

"*Could* be Doc or Slow Wolf." Larry spoke almost desperately, as though trying to convince himself. "Just some hassle they're caught up in. Might be one of 'em's gonna stand trial and the lawyer figures I can help his case, somethin' like that."

"More likely Slow Wolf than Doc," Stretch suggested. "The chief'd name us if he needed help. But Doc? We like him, but he don't like us. Every time we run into that dude . . . "

"He gets mad at us," said Larry, grinning reminiscently. "Says we should stay far clear of him and we're just a blame nuisance to him. Good ol' Doc. He'll just never change."

As they made the ascent, letting their animals choose their own pace, Stretch warned, "Better face it. For all we know, Mister Crouse never heard of Doc Beaumont or our old Injun buddy. Why he sent, for you — that's a question we can t even guess."

"So why *wouldn't* I be curious?" growled Larry.

"Yup," nodded Stretch. "You got a right."

They were half-way up the grade when a westbound train passed them. The engineer was tending his controls, his partner shovelling fuel, with the conductor lounging in the open side doorway of the baggage car. The conductor waved to the horsemen. They returned his wave and, soon,

58

the train reached the summit and was lost from dew.

Some twenty minutes later, the tall men finished their climb and found themselves atop a mesa. The wind wasn't strong, just a caressing, cooling breeze, and the mesa by no means barren. Timber a short distance to their right. They wheeled their mounts off the trail and headed over there, confident they would find a clearing, which they did.

Stretch appointed himself cook. While he broke out provisions and gathered wood for a fire, Larry looked to the feeding and watering of the horses. When their meal was ready for eating, they satisfied their appetites and, mutually realizing the futility of speculation, voiced no hunches as to why a lawyer named Crouse so urgently needed the presence of a footloose outlaw-fighter named Valentine. Nor did they discuss the reason for their forced stay in Gibbsville. They had, as so often in the past, stumbled upon a stagecoach hold-up in progress and reacted instinctively. Resenting their intrusion, the robbers had rashly opened fire on them and gotten the worst of the ensuing shootout. Messrs Valentine and Emerson had co-operated as demanded and testified at the trials of the miscreants. It was one of many such incidents in their hectic past and that's where it belonged, in the past, so they had forgotten it.

Having finished his coffee, and for want of something better to do, Larry took his field glasses from his saddlebag and trudged through the trees to the north timberline. From there, he scanned the terrain to the northwest. He adjusted the focus for a closer appraisal of all he could see. It was impressive.

He called to his partner to join him and offered the binoculars.

"Take a look," he urged. "In our travels, we've seen a lot of great cattle country, but this beats all."

Born and raised in the Texan Panhandle, both of them the offspring of ranchers, it was instinctive to them. Drifters they were, tumbleweeds who had become versatile, turning their hands to all manner of chores to earn an honest dollar when their joint bankroll needed boosting, but still cattlemen at heart.

Stretch used the glasses and loosed a low whistle. "Man, oh man."

"Even from this far off, you can tell that's prime stock," drawled Larry.

"Helluva big herd," observed Stretch. "And all that grazeland. Hell, must be the greenest range in all Arizona." As he returned the glasses, he asked. "You suppose that's all one spread?"

"Might be," said Larry. "Storekeeper back in Gibbsville talked of a big outfit in this territory, the Gelbart ranch. That could be it — or more likely just a piece of it, just as much as we're seein',"

"With all that greenery," Stretch remarked when they returned to their camp, "you can bet your double-cinched saddle there'd be no scrawny

61

dogies on Gelbart range. Not like down south, this side of the Rio Bravo."

"Where it's hotter and dryer, yeah," agreed Larry. "I guess this is the best part of the Arizona Territory."

They packed gear, killed the fire and remounted to resume their westward journey and, before they began the descent from the mesa, Larry again produced his field glasses. He didn't call a halt, studying the area ahead on the move.

"See the town?" asked Stretch.

"Big'un," nodded Larry. "Has to be Hart City. Yeah, big. And it won't be dark when we get there. Full hour before sundown maybe."

"Not much farther to go, not much longer for you to wait for some answers," Stretch said encouragingly.

Around 4.15 p.m., with the big town dead ahead, they noted the network of stockyards south of the railroad depot, the residential streets angling off Hart City's main street and more than a few buildings all of three storeys tall. Momentarily disgruntled, Stretch remarked it looked to be almost as sizeable as Denver; the drifters were allergic to towns big enough to be called frontier cities. The bigger the city — and they had seen Chicago and San Francisco — the greater their sense of not belonging.

"When we ride in, we're makin' straight for Crouse's office," decided Larry. "You're right, beanpole. Not our kind of town. Too much like Denver, Santa Fe, Carson City and all them other hustlin' places. Whatever this lawyer wants from me, let's hope we can take care of it fast."

"I'm with you, runt," muttered Stretch. "Hart City's likely fine for folks that live here, but no place for us pilgrims."

Reaching the railroad depot, they swung north to walk their animals into Main Street. Now that they were here, the memory of bustling Denver was even stronger. It seemed every citizen visible was in a hurry to get somewhere.

They saw few dawdlers. The passer-by they questioned was moving briskly, but did pause long enough to oblige.

"Gordon Crouse's office? Easy to find. West side of the street and a block and a half up. Look out for Winkler's photography place, a double storey. Crouse's office is on the second floor. You'll see the steps."

"Muchas gracias," acknowledged Larry.

They found the Winkler establishment, swung down, tied their mounts to the hitchrail and made for the flight of wooden stairs. Climbing them, they came to a landing with a closed door to which the lawyer's shingle was fixed.

"Well, we've found him," Stretch remarked as Larry knocked.

Invited to enter, they opened the door and moved into Crouse's office. He at once rose from his desk chair, grinned in relief and offered his hand.

"Mister Valentine and, of course, Mister Emerson. What a welcome sight you are. Gordon Crouse. Thanks for coming."

They shook hands with him. He gestured them to chairs and declared, as so many others had, that he'd have known them anywhere. Newspaper photographers had captured an excellent likeness of them. They had heard all this before.

Larry nudged his Stetson off his brow, fished out his makings and, while building a smoke, looked the lawyer in the eye and asked gruffly, "Mister Crouse, what the hell am I doin' here?"

3

Extra Aces

GORDON CROUSES'S preamble began while he filled a straight-stemmed pipe from the humidor on his desk.

"You're confused, Mister Valentine, and that's only to be expected. You didn't know the late Edward Jesse Gelbart, but maybe you've heard of him?"

"All I've heard is the name," said Larry, lighting his quirley. "Owns — I mean owned — a big cattle spread hereabouts, right?"

"The Lone Star Ranch," offered Crouse.

"Well, he gave his spread a right fine name," commented Stretch. "And I'll bet his brand's a star." Crouse nodded. "Good figurin', huh runt?

With a runnin' iron, how could a rustler change such a brand?"

"Couldn't," agreed Larry. "Was the old feller . . . ?"

"A Texan, yes," said Crouse. "He married here. The late Sadie Gelbart was a fine woman, well respected as her husband was. There was issue of the marriage, a daughter and two sons."

"Bueno," frowned Larry. "But you still ain't tellin' me why . . ."

"They're waiting at Lone Star now," said Crouse. "The daughter, Elva, is Mrs Morton Sherwood of Sacramento. Her husband is with her. They're the parents of my late client's three grandchildren. The elder brother, Jesse, is also married. He and his wife are from San Francisco. The younger brother, Vernon, is a bachelor, He had to make the longest journey, as Chicago is his home city."

"They're waitin' . . . ?" prodded Larry.

"For the reading of their late father's last will and testament," explained

Crouse. "To be more specific, Mister Valentine, I could not read the will to them without your being present."

"Larry's got to be there?" blinked Stretch.

"Mister Gelbart's strict instruction to me," nodded Crouse. "It's unlikely I'll ever have a wealthier client. I enjoyed his trust and am his executor. Therefore, it's my professional duty to ensure his wishes are complied with."

"I already told you I didn't know him," mumbled a perplexed Larry.

"This much I can tell you," said Crouse. "One of the old gentleman's greatest regrets is you never met." He scratched a match, got his pipe working and aimed a smile at Stretch. "That, of course, means both of you. He spoke of you often, always confiding his hope you'd come to this territory. Had that happened, I'm sure he'd have insisted on your being his guests for as long as you wished. You were great favorites of his."

"We just drift," shrugged Larry.

"And do our doggonedest to stay out of trouble," sighed Stretch.

"He admired your achievements," declared Crouse. "I sense you resent your reputation. Fame has its disadvantages?"

"And then some," Larry assured him.

"I can imagine, and I sympathize," said Crouse. "But, if you won't think me too personal . . ."

"Talk as personal as you want," invited Stretch. "We ain't special, and we'd feel some easier if you skipped the Misters. My ol' buddy here, he's Larry, and I'm Stretch."

"Sounds friendlier," Larry suggested.

"Fine," said Crouse. "I'm rarely addressed as Gordon. My wife and all our friends call me Gordy."

"So far, we don't think you're bein' too personal, so what were you about to say?" asked Larry.

"Just that, in my opinion, and certainly Ed Gelbart's opinion, you're entitled to resent your reputation," said Crouse, "I realize it's been a drawback to you at times, but you should never be ashamed of it. You could be described as dangerous, but only to law-breakers, never to honest folk."

"Sometimes, that's no comfort at all," grouched Stretch.

"You're curious, naturally," Crouse remarked to Larry. "I wish I could satisfy your curiosity here. and now, but I can't. There's a limit to how much I can tell you before the reading of the will."

"So what *can* you tell us here and now?" demanded Larry.

"Precious little, but try me," said Crouse. "There maybe a question I can answer without betraying my client's trust."

"He was old?" said Larry.

"Well on in years," said Crouse.

"And — uh — maybe a little . . . ?" Larry raised finger to temple.

The lawyer shook his head emphatically.

"Never feeble-minded, Larry. In full possession of his faculties till the moment of his death. His physician

70

will confirm that. Lew Richmond was a close friend and with him at the end, also the foreman, Duff Wheatley, and the housekeeper, Señora Bedoya. Always loyal, the Bedoyas. They're the house servants."

"He wanted I should be there for the will-readin', but you don't know why," mused Larry.

"I know why, but can't tell you," Crouse said carefully.

"I guess, after the will's read, his young'uns're gonna be plenty rich," said Larry. No reply from Crouse. "All right, just *how* big is Lone Star, and when're you gonna read the will?"

"At the last tally, according to Duff Wheatley, Lone Star was grazing all of fifteen thousand head — prime stock," said Crouse.

"Holy Hannah!" breathed Stretch.

"Lone Star really prospered these past fifteen years," Crouse told them. "Not like the old days. No trail drives to a railhead hundreds of miles distant. Riding in, you must've noticed the loading pens. Nowadays, after spring round-up, cattle buyers from Chicago and the west coast come to Hart City — dozens of them. Sales are negotiated here, bills of sale signed, cheques written and banked. Lone Star stock goes to only the highest bidders and pay-herds are driven only from home range to the stockyards. That's progress."

"Sure is." Larry was impressed.

"For reading the will, the appropriate time would be tomorrow morning," said Crouse. "I'll have a courier take a note to Mrs Sherwood informing her we should arrive by ten. It was the old man's wish that you and Stretch be accommodated at Lone Star as soon as possible after your arrival, but I'm not in favor of reading the will tonight. Tomorrow morning would be better."

The trouble-shooters traded frowns.

"We're supposed to bunk out there — with his young'uns?" challenged Stretch.

"You'll be comfortable I assure you,"

smiled Crouse. "I doubt you've ever seen a ranch-house to compare with the home Ed Gelbart built for his family. It's massive, a double-storey sandstone hacienda style. Ample room for you."

"How — uh — how many hired hands?" asked Larry.

"Well, there are four house servants, the Bedoyas and their daughters," said Crouse. "As for the ranch-hands . . . " He paused, mentally calculating. "I'd say, excluding wranglers, the chuck-boss, the blacksmith and Duff Wheatley, three dozen. That's a conservative estimate. There are four other ranches in Hart County but — I'm sure you're convinced now — Lone Star is the biggest."

"Seems like old Ed did everything big," remarked Larry.

"But from a humble beginning." The lawyer became wistful; plainly, he had lost a rich client, but also an admired friend. "Came west from Texas long years ago with his buddy Duff and less than a hundred dollars in his

73

pockets, did some gambling en route, and that's when his luck changed for the better. By the time he reached this territory, he'd bought good breed stock and could afford to buy land. That's how Lone Star got started. He married, prospered and became a key figure of the Hart County community — he had amassed a fortune. His luck changed, but he didn't. He was always the same casual Ed Gelbart, shrewd, patient and never a braggart. You'd have liked him and, as I've said, he was fond of you both."

"So he was a good ol' boy, no denyin' that," said Stretch. "But we're still all mixed up."

"I don't savvy why he . . . " began Larry.

"He wrote you a note," offered Crouse. "I imagine it will explain many things to you, Larry."

"Fine," Larry said eagerly. "C'mon, I want to read it so I can make sense of all this."

"You'll be reading it, but not

rightaway," said Crouse. "Another of my sworn obligations to him. It's addressed to you, sealed and in my safe. Under your name, he clearly wrote 'Not to be opened until four days after the reading of my will.' So I can't give it to you before then."

"By damn, he sure liked to act mysterious," Stretch commented.

"I'm sure he had his reasons," declared Crouse. "That old gentleman was never an eccentric."

Larry shrugged and got to his feet; Stretch followed his example, suggesting, "Best we stable our critters and find a hotel."

"If you can meet me here eight-thirty tomorrow morning, we should reach Lone Star at the time I've nominated," Crouse told them. "We'll be expected. I'll compose a note at once and have somebody deliver it to Mrs Sherwood."

From the doorway, Larry looked back at him and put a last question.

"How do they feel about it, Mrs Sherwood and her brothers? Maybe they never heard of my partner and me."

"I was not at liberty to divulge your names," said Crouse. "I could only inform them the will could not be read before the arrival of another person. Jesse and his brother Vern are naturally curious, their sister and her husband even more so." He shrugged helplessly. "Better be prepared, Larry. The Sherwoods are also indignant — and somewhat hostile about the delay."

"We'll remember to beg their pardon," said Larry.

The trouble-shooters toted their gear to the hotel closest the stable where they left their horses, checked into a ground-floor double, took turns to bathe and change and, by supper-time, were working their way through a fulsome meal in the hotel's dining-room — and still confused.

"Don't know much, do we?" Stretch reflected. "Only thing we know for a fact is we were wrong about old buddies of ours. Wasn't on account of Doc the lawyer sent for you, Slow Wolf neither."

"No," nodded Larry. "Somethin' else; It's real nice old Ed was Texan and thought kindly of us, but why'd he finagle us into comin' to Hart City?"

"You're askin' *me*?" winced Stretch.

"No use frettin' and wonderin'," Larry decided some time later. They had finished eating and were drinking coffee. "Manana's another day. Meantime, the night's young and I'd as soon find a Poker party than flop in this hotel."

"Friendly saloon sounds good to me," said Stretch. "Slip me fifty from our roll and I'll play the roulette layout, maybe shoot craps."

Throughout their wanderings in the years following the end of the Civil War, Larry had been their banker, the custodian of their finances. No special reason beyond the fact that he owned a wallet and his partner didn't. He dug out the wallet and passed Stretch five $10 bills. He was a skilled poker

77

player. Their luck at games of chance kept them solvent. When the luck failed them, they worked to build another stake; such was their well-established routine.

From the hotel, they sauntered the long and wide, brightly lit main street and eventually settled for Holly Orban's Lucky Deal Saloon in the midtown area. It looked to be just right for their present needs, a big place and busy, providing gambling facilities, good quality liquor served by two barkeeps, four Mexican musicians and percentage-girls prettier than most.

Housemen presided at all games of chance, including the poker tables. The dealer at the table to which Larry gravitated was Clint Elphick, a dapper, blond, impassive individual. Stretch joined the optimists at the roulette layout and, after dropping $20, abandoned roulette in favor of nursing a shot of rye on a bench-seat by the south wall. Just a feeling, a hunch. Not being mechanically minded, he was in no position to voice his suspicion the wheel was rigged to ensure it operated at a profit, mainly for the Lucky Deal; it was just a hunch and, like his partner, he always went with his hunches.

When a Hart County identity of earlier years entered the saloon, few patrons recognized him. Vern Gelbart's only concession to his return to the West was his headgear; a Stetson had replaced his homburg. He paused inside the batwings, glanced about the bar-room and sighted two unforgettable locals sharing a corner table. With a bland grin, he moved across to them, drew out a chair and seated himself.

"As I live and breathe," exclaimed Dr Richmond. "Young Vern!"

"And he never looked better," Joe Mirram observed as he offered his hand.

Vern shook with them. The newspaperman signalled one of the girls to take his order. He requested a short bourbon. The girl obliged and was handsomely tipped.

"Your health, gentlemen," he offered, raising his glass. "And, speaking of appearances, neither of you has changed a bit." They sampled their drinks. He gave them Havanas, lit one for himself and said warmly, "I'm not just being polite. Doc, you don't seem to age, and it's been quite a time since I last saw you. Same with you, Mister Mirram."

"Well, it's the way we earn our daily bread maybe," smiled Mirram. "No aspect of the practice of medicine, no case he has to attend, could worry Doc. He's seen it all."

"And Joe has settled into just as cosy a rut," said Richmond. "His working routine is regular, as is mine. Stability, Vern. There is much to be said for stability."

"Better keep that in mind, young feller," Mirram good-humoredly advised. "Show business has its ups and downs and could cause premature aging."

"True enough," agreed Vern. "But I believe it's all a matter of enjoying what we do, and I certainly enjoy my

80

chosen profession."

"Ed Gelbart's younger son — an actor," mused the medic "Who'd have foreseen it?"

"I suppose many of Dad's old cohorts are just as surprised that Jesse studied accountancy," said Vern.

"You speak of your brother and I'm at once reminded of your sister-in-law," frowned Richmond. "Damned unfortunate, her bronchial condition. Kind of ailment that sometimes has lasting effects. How is the young lady coping with life at Lone Star?'

"Splendidly," grinned Vern. "Trudy seems to be gaining strength, blooming in fact. She's obviously feeling better and looking better. Jesse is much relieved, and so am I."

"One personal question coming up," said Mirram. "If I'm out of line, I'll apologize."

"Feel free," offered Vern.

"Do you find your brother-in-law as easy to get along with as your sister-in-law?" asked Mirram.

81

Poker-faced, Vern replied, "That's not humanly possible. Trudy's amiable and appealing and the perfect wife for Jesse. Mort's a blustering curmudgeon and the perfect husband for Elva." He winked as he added, "If either of you quote me, I'll deny I ever uttered those words."

The medico and the *Journal* editor traded appreciative grins. Old Ed's passing was a tragedy, but had brought his children home. It was good to have jaunty Vern on the local scene again, even if temporarily.

Came now the distraction. The musicians had stopped performing in mid-chorus. Wary glances were aimed at a poker table. With all his poker savvy, it hadn't taken Larry long to detect the sharper's tricks practiced by Clint Elphick. The man was deft, he conceded, expert at sleight of hand. The other players hadn't noticed. He had.

The sudden tension was caused by his calmly voiced accusation.

"Elphick's your name, right? Well

now, Elphick, I got to say you're good, real good. Matter of fact, I'd rate you one of the slickest sharpers every gypped me. But that's what you are. A sharper."

Elphick replied, with no show of alarm, "Go see an eye doctor, cowboy. You don't see as clearly as you claim."

"I'm keen-sighted," Larry assured him.

"You couldn't be," countered Elphick. "Whatever you think you've seen, you *didn't* see it. And sore losers aren't welcome in the Lucky Deal."

"When I lose in a fair-square game, I never complain," growled Larry. "I'm only a sore loser when a dealer cheats me."

"I don't take kindly to your accusation," Elphick said warningly.

"And I don't take kindly to your double dealin'," retorted Larry. The other players were becoming edgy; Larry kept his gaze fixed on Elphick. "As well as slippin' yourself a card or two from under the deck, you got hideaways inside your sleeves."

A nerve twitched high on Elphick's left cheekbone. He called loudly to his boss.

"Mister Orban, we have a sore loser, a trouble-maker!"

Holly Orban promptly materialized and Stretch, on his feet now, tried to recall when last he'd seen so much blubber. The saloonkeeper was around five feet ten and uncommonly fat, his belly massive, his blotchy face moon-shaped and double-chinned. Thumbs tucked in the armholes of a paisley-patterned vest, he announced, "All my patrons know I run an honest place and that I don't tolerate trouble-makers." His pig like eyes fastened on Larry. "I'm barring you from the Lucky Deal as of right now."

"You're entitled," shrugged Larry. "So I'll be glad to leave. But not without every dollar I've been cheated of."

He was genuinely surprised when Elphick's temper flared; up till now

84

he'd had the dealer pegged for a cool operator. The backhander Elphick swung at him stung his face. Dumb mistake, as he was soon made to realize. Larry retaliated by abruptly quitting his chair, rounding the table and jerking the sharper upright by his coatcollar. Elphick hastily produced a Remington derringer. Larry wrested it from his hand, tossed it to the floor, then tore his coat off.

Shocked, the other players watched Larry shake the garment. High cards, most of them aces, fell from the sleeves. Orban was about to begin another speech when the roulette, blackjack and faro supervisors began converging on Larry. One of the barkeeps vaulted the counter, grinning maliciously and hefting a mean-looking club. There was a sudden scatter, the hired girls making for the staircase, patrons retreating to the side walls, some quitting the premises. The doctor, the newspaperman and the youngest Gelbart stayed put.

Hustling to intercept his partner's would-be assailants, Stretch called an appeal.

"Let's not get warlike, gents. My buddy and me don't want no trouble."

It didn't seem likely his appeal would be heeded, but he felt compelled to voice it.

Larry had to turn his back on Elphick to face the men advancing on him. His head rang from the punch thrown at him from behind. Grimacing, he whirled and jabbed with his left, and Elphick backstepped three paces and collapsed with his nose bloody. It was the saloonkeeper's turn to give in to temper.

"Throw those saddletramps out of here!" he ordered.

His dealers attacked and immediately began paying the penalty. The roulette man swung at Larry, missed and was sent hurtling ail the way to the bar by a powerful uppercut. If Stretch hadn't thrown a sidelong glance to the back bar mirror, he might have fallen victim to a paralyzing blow. The barkeep's club was swinging, his target the nape of Stretch's neck.

Stretch ducked as low as he could, almost to his knees. The barkeep was bulky, but the taller Texan seemed unaware of his weight. When he came upright, the barkeep was helpless in his grip and being raised shoulder-high. Stretch threw him as easily he would a half-filled grainsack and, yelling, he soared over the bar to slam against shelves laden with bottles and glasses; the shelves and their contents went down with him. Stretch now sidestepped, and not a moment too soon. The kick aimed at his crotch by the blackjack dealer missed. His right fist didn't. It exploded in the blackjack man's face and put him to the floor with a resounding thud.

The faro man and another poker dealer were crowding Larry, landing blows but taking more punishment than they could hand out. One was sent crashing onto a vacated table by a round house left. Larry's right started the other reeling away to collide with Elphick, who had begun rising. Both men flopped and stayed down.

The battle had been violent, but short, lasting only a few minutes. Side by side, the Texans eyed other dealers and the visible barkeep. The other barkeep rose dazedly, slivers of glass falling from his head and shoulders, his shirt stained by liquor from smashed bottles. His colleague wisely decided he'd make no hostile move toward the Texans; it wasn't worth what Holly Orban paid him. From above the stairs, the girls gaped at the scene.

"Any other fool jumps us, we'll defend ourselves," Larry warned everybody. "Hang onto that thought, okay?" He turned to the other players. "Gents, I'm takin' mine from the pot, every dollar I calculate I got gypped of. And I'm invitin' you to do likewise."

"Sounds fair to me," one of the men muttered.

Orban was red-faced, temporarily

speechless, when the players retrieved their losses. The tension increased when two lawmen came barging in, the smaller of them brandishing a shotgun. Will Apley, sheriff of Hart County, was of unimpressive build, sallow complexioned with pale blue eyes and a receding chin. The other lawman, a deputy, Jay Elhurst by name, was burly, flatnosed and heavy-jawed.

It was all so familiar to the trouble-shooters, this aftermath to a clash with a cardsharp and his colleagues. Stretch tended to be fatalistic about it, Larry too, but not on this occasion. Fury still gripped him. Same old routine, he was thinking. The fat man would demand that two strangers, trouble-makers, be locked up muy pronto. Who would support the Texans? Nobody, he supposed. Same old story. The law siding with a local big shot. Well, the hell with them all. Not this time. Not so they'd notice.

"Taken long enough for you to show up, Will," scowled Orban.

"Got here as fast as I . . . " began Apley.

"Look at what these saddletramps did to my employees," fumed Orban. "The sore loser accused Elphick of cheating. They started a brawl, caused ail this damage. Go on, Will. Do your duty."

"You . . . " Larry glowered at Apley and pointed to the levelled shotgun, "keep that thing uncocked. And you . . . " He turned to cold-eye Orban, "you're a fat slob and a liar."

"Mind your mouth, feller!" chided Apley. "That's no way to talk to a town councilman, a respected alderman of this community!" Stretch suddenly stopped being fatalistic. Contemptuously indicating Orban, he challenged the lawman.

"You tellin' us there's citizens *respect* that tub of lard?"

"They're riff-raff!" gasped Orban. "Regular clients of this saloon know I run an honest house, no sharpers on my payroll! What're you waiting for,

Will? Arrest these trail-bums!"

The big deputy was stroking his jowls and studying the tall men thoughtfully, and Apley about to cock his shotgun, when Doc Richmond stepped to the fore tagged by a dapper young man and the editor of the *Journal*.

"Since everybody else seems dumb-struck, I guess it's up to me to clarify the situation," he calmly told Apley. He nodded to Larry. "This man and the others in the poker game dealt by Elphick were being cheated. He proved it by removing Elphick's coat. If you care to take a closer look, Sheriff, you'll see the high cards that fell from the sleeves."

"Now, Doc, you oughtn't interfere," complained Orban.

"Call it interference if you wish — that's your privilege," shrugged the medico. "But damned if I'll stay silent and tolerate a blatant injustice. Another point, Sheriff. Neither stranger resorted to violence before he was attacked. They didn't instigate the brawl. And I trust I needn't remind you of a man's right to defend himself."

Though nervous, Mirram spoke up. "Unless they're blind, everybody present must've seen what we saw," he told Apley. "The dealer did cheat, and he struck the first blow, also pulled a sneak-gun. Doc's word ought to be good enough for you, Sheriff. And mine."

"Mine also — I should hope." Vern smiled his bland smile and moved forward to stand beside Richmond and the newspaperman. "I doubt we three were the only witnesses. Have I changed so much?" He glanced around. "Does nobody recognize me? Gelbart's the name, Vernon Gelbart. You weren't in office when I left this territory, Sheriff, but I'm sure the Gelbart name is well known to you. Also the tradition established by my beloved father — a Gelbart's word is his bond."

Apley faltered. Orban gnawed at his underlip and did some fast thinking. The other victims of Elphick's double dealing finally decided they should speak up; they confirmed Richmond's statement. Some onlookers followed suit, now recalling the taller Texan's vain appeal to the houseman threatening his partner.

If it were physically possible, Holly Orban would have kicked himself for his show of temper. He was losing face, and knew it. Desperately, he raised his voice again, declaring, "I'm a fair-minded man as everybody knows. It seems I'm mistaken — because Doc Richmond's word is good enough for me any time. And, of course, the word of any Gelbart. I'm shocked that a member of my staff was caught cheating." He pointed sternly to Elphick. "Get up to my office. You're through here. I'm gonna pay you off and, if you know what's good for you, you'll leave Hart City this very night and never return."

Some, but not all of the onlookers accepted that announcement as proof that the fat man was as indignant as he seemed. Elphick climbed the stairs, dabbing at his nose with a handkerchief. The Texans lost interest in Apley and fell in behind the three men making for the batwings, Doc Richmond and his companions.

A short distance from the Lucky Deal, they paused. The trouble-shooters thanked their supporters. Richmond responded by performing introductions.

"You already heard young Vern identify himself. This is Joe Mirram, editor of the newspaper here. I'm Doctor Lewis Richmond, at your service — but I hope not. Two other doctors resident here, and they're welcome to those losers at Orban's, the fools who you . . . "

"Beat the living daylights out of," Vern enthused with a gleeful grin.

"Well, we're obliged to you gents," Larry acknowledged. "This here's my partner, Emerson, called Stretch. I'm Valentine, called Larry."

"I know," Mirram said carefully.

"Uh huh, you would," nodded

Stretch. "Bein' a newspaper scribbler."

"A member of the profession you despise," admitted Mirram.

"We owe you," said Larry. "So relax. Man does us a kindness, we appreciate it."

"I've heard of you of course," frowned Richmond.

"Who hasn't?" Vern was studying the tall men in a friendly way. "I suppose you're aware you're not unknown in Chicago? The city papers often run reports of your actions against law-breakers. What a hectic life!"

"We've seen Chicago," said Larry. "We were there once, but that was many a long year ago."

"Back when a big piece of Chicago caught fire," recalled Stretch. He hastened to add, "But it wasn't us. We didn't start that fire."

This earnest assurance amused the medico. Mirram almost grinned. Vern couldn't suppress a chuckle.

Richmond bade the Texans goodnight and remarked to Mirram, "I'll walk you back to your office, Joe." A cordial nod for Vern. "Good seeing you again, young feller."

"My pleasure," said Vern. Then, as Richmond and Mirram moved away, he remarked to the Texans, "Thought I'd ride in to renew memories of the old town. Didn't anticipate there'd be so much excitement. The way you warriors defend yourselves is, to say the least, impressive. I think I'll ride home now."

"Ride safe," said Larry.

"It's a good trail, I selected a good horse and I was born at Lone Star," said Vern. "I've been away quite a few years, but nothing changes. I could find my way home to the ranch blindfolded."

Larry had resisted the urge to inform Vern Gelbart he'd be seeing them again and quite soon, no later than 10 a.m. of the morrow. Maybe some of Gordy Crouse's reticence was rubbing off on him. He and Stretch returned to their hotel while, in his office above the

96

bar-room, Orban gave Elphick a wad of banknotes.

"Sorry to lose you, Clint," he muttered. "You know the score. George and me, we can't afford for the suckers to turn on us. Something like this happens, we have to cover ourselves. Bad for business, you know?"

"Yeah, sure." Elphick counted the money and pocketed it. "I'll be headed for Garcia Wells soon as I pack, and you know you don't have to remind me to keep my mouth shut."

"Of course I don't," nodded the fat man. "That's our arrangement with all the boys we hire, George and me."

"First time, Holly," frowned Elphick.

"Never happened before," agreed Orban.

"You're one of the best. Haven't I always said it?"

"That damn saddlebum must have eyes like an eagle," complained Elphick. "I wasn't careless, never am."

"Only explanation I can think of is he's older than he looks — and experienced," said Orban.

"You can never guess how much poker-savvy some jaspers have. For all we know, that sonofabitch could've learned every trick in the game from an old pro."

Doc Richmond's first move, after accompanying Mirram into his office, took him by surprise. When he seated himself in his desk chair, Richmond checked his pulse. He then took his stethoscope from his bag and checked the newspaperman's heart beat.

"Why . . . ?" began Mirram.

"Call it professional preoccupation with the health of an old friend," said Richmond. "Joe, you've watched other bar-room brawls, but this one seemed special to you. I've never seen you so excited. Your eyes were popping."

"Well," Mirram said uneasily, "there was a reason."

4

Surprise, Surprise

RICHMOND replaced his stethoscope in his bag and made himself comfortable in the chair fronting the desk. The newspaperman lit a cigar and asked, "Find anything I ought to worry about?"

"Pulse and heartbeat normal — now," said Richmond. "You've had time to calm yourself. But, while those drifters were bouncing Orban's hired help all around the bar-room, you were a mighty nerved up observer. There was a reason, you say?"

"Doc, we know things aren't — well — the way they ought to be in this town," said Mirram.

Taxes are too high, we all say," nodded Richmond. "And it's now obvious the gluttonous Holly Orban had at least one cardsharp on his payroll. About the tax rises, we all complain, but then Hart City is a prosperous town and it has to be conceded our administrators have made certain improvements." He eyed Mirram enquiringly. "What is it, Joe? Is there something in particular troubling you?"

"Right now, I'm just curious about something," muttered Mirram. "I wouldn't say I'm troubled. Just expectant."

"Impossible." The medico tried to lighten the mood with a jest. "You're a hundred percent male."

Mirram grinned briefly.

"Sure I am. Ask my wife. She'll vouch for it."

"What is it you expect — or don't you want to discuss it with me?" prodded Richmond.

"I'll confide in you any time — you know that," said Mirram. "Because I can always rely on your discretion. We have a private conversation, you don't blab it around, anything we've said."

"So," frowned Richmond. "What's on your mind?"

"You asked am I expecting something," said Mirram. "I certainly am, Doc. One helluva commotion. A lot of upheaval. We recently lost a damn fine man, Ed Gelbart, who happened to be the only Texan in this territory. Except for Duff Wheatley of course."

"And?"

"And now, only a short time after he's laid to rest, *they* show up."

"Those drifters?"

"They're Texan, Doc. Some coincidence, wouldn't you say? And Valentine's more than a fiddle-footed drifter. He's known to be quite a detective, as smart an investigator as any Pinkerton."

"You're getting excited again," chided medico. "Joe, the old man wasn't a murder victim I was his doctor. I signed the death certificate. Natural causes. To be specific his heart just gave up. He was no youngster and he'd lived hard; stayed active long after he'd become a millionaire."

"I know old Ed wasn't murdered," Mirram said impatiently. "It's the coincidence factor. *That's* what intrigues me. An old Texan dies. He was a legend in his own time . . . "

"All cattle barons become famous, no matter where they were born," shrugged Richmond.

"Valentine and Emerson are just as famous," stressed Mirram. "Ed Gelbart was a Texan, and *they're* Texan."

"Why so apprehensive, Joe?" demanded Richmond. "They're rough men, I agree. Certainly proved it just now, but there was good reason for Valentine's hostility. We're his witnesses. The dealer was a cardsharp and . . . "

"That upheaval at the Lucky Deal was, by comparison, an insignificant disagreement," sighed Mirram.

"In comparison to what?" asked Richmond.

"To the *greater* upheaval," Mirram said quietly. "With those two in Hart

County, it's inevitable. We can expect turmoil such as this territory has never known. And violence — bloodshed maybe."

"I hope you're wrong," said Richmond.

"*I* hope I'm wrong," retorted Mirram.

When Vern Gelbart returned to the big ranch, a hired hand took charge of the horse he'd used. His brother and sister-in-law were in side-by-side chairs on the ground-floor porch, savoring the cooling night breeze before calling it a day.

They had news for him.

"The lawyer sent word," Jesse offered as his brother joined them. "Reading of Dad's will, Vern. Ten o'clock tomorrow morning. The unknown beneficiary . . . "

"Unknown to us," interjected Trudy.

" . . . must have arrived," finished Jesse. "Crouse will bring him here and, within a half-hour, we'll no longer he wondering how Dad's estate is to be divided."

"At last Sis and Mort will be satisfied," remarked Vern. "Well, as satisfied as one may expect of them."

"We shouldn't be too hard on them," pleaded Trudy. "It must be a worry, being separated from their children."

"Patience was never our sister's long suit, Trudy," said Vern. "As for our niece and nephews, they're in good hands, surrounded by servants dedicated to their welfare."

"You didn't stay long in town," said Jesse.

"Not a long visit, but eventful," Vern told him. "I had a little reunion with Joe Mirram and Doc Richmond in a saloon, a place called the Lucky Deal. It was good seeing them again. Incredible the way they never change."

"They're older," insisted Jesse.

"But not showing their years," said Vern.

"Eventful you say?" prodded Jesse.

"We were witnesses to a pitched brawl," said Vern.

"How terrible," frowned Trudy.

"Well, it wasn't for your eyes," grinned Vern. "Personally, I enjoyed it, and I'm sure Doc did. Quite a performance. And, speaking of the passing of the years, the victors of that spectacular affray are as active, as formidable as twenty-year-olds. You'll have heard of them, Jesse. Their fame spreads far and wide. Valentine and Emerson, two of the wandering kind with a penchant for violence."

"Those two?" frowned Jesse. "*Still* in action? I'm surprised they've survived so long."

"On my count, they were set upon by no fewer than six adversaries," chuckled Vern. "Employees of the Lucky Deal who, by the time the last blow was struck, were in a somewhat reduced condition. Oh, yes, much the worse for wear. And, by contrast, those trouble-shooters were fighting fit and ready for more of the same. Great fellows. I have to admire them."

"Who are they?" Trudy was curious. "And what exactly is a trouble-shooter?"

"A couple of drifters much appreciated by the Press, honey, because their exploits make good copy," said Jesse. "As for a definition of the term 'trouble-shooter', what do you say, little brother?"

"Valentine and his crony might best be described as independent warriors, mercenaries perhaps," said Vern. "They seem to be continually at war with outlaws. They've settled a great many crises, find common ground with law-abiding folk and are chivalrous to ladies of the frontier. I had a brief conversation with them and was intrigued. Roughnecks they may be, but they have, I believe, the instincts of true gentlemen."

Jesse checked his watch.

"Bedtime," he decided. "Big day tomorrow."

★ ★ ★

At 8.20 next morning, Gordon Crouse unlocked his safe and withdrew the thick envelope containing the last will and testament of Edward Jesse Gelbart.

106

His nerves were steady. Having drawn up the will, he was anticipating a shock reaction out at Lone Star, but was more amused than apprehensive.

He stowed the will in his satchel and, before re-locking the safe, frowned at two other envelopes, the one he would hand Larry Valentine four days from now, the one he was to open if and when a certain event should occur. After locking the safe, he cocked an ear to a clip-clop of hooves. Those Texans arriving early, he guessed. By now, Larry Valentine's curiosity must be giving him hell. He donned his hat and, toting his satchel, locked up and descended to the street.

This morning, he had not walked from his home to his office. His buggy awaited out front, the tall men sitting their mounts beside it, smoking their after-breakfast cigarettes and nodding to him.

"Fair morning for it," he remarked, boarding his rig. "On our way to the ranch-house, you'll enjoy a clear view

107

of Lone Star range. Part of it anyway. There's so much of it." He clucked to the buggy horse and drove off, the Texans flanking him. "I missed last night's fracas at the Orban saloon. You seem none the worse for it."

"Word travels just as fast in big towns as small towns," muttered Larry, as they travelled north along Main.

"Doc Richmond paid us an early call," the lawyer explained. "Adeline, my wife, is expecting our third child. Not due just yet, but Doc Richmond's conscientious, keeps a close watch on maternity cases."

"Hope Mrs Crouse ain't poorly," Stretch said politely.

"Doing well," said Crouse. "We're hoping for a boy this time."

Out of the county seat, they pressed on along the trail to Lone Star. The Texans had viewed some of the vast Gelbart acreage from a distance and through field glasses. Soon, they were crossing it, the trail snaking across verdant graze, a thousand head or more steers in sight, here and there a herder nudging bunch-quitters clear of mesquite patches. Cattle baron, they were thinking. When a man owns so much prime graze, runs a herd tallying to 15,000 or more, you don't call him a rancher; he's a cattle baron. They were a mite overawed and looked it. This didn't surprise Crouse; he was well aware they sprang from cattle country.

Larry thought to mention they'd met a Gelbart last night.

"Sociable young feller."

"Vern, the youngest of the three children," nodded Crouse. "Doc told me. You didn't . . . ?"

"Nope," grunted Larry. "Didn't say 'see you tomorrow'. Figured you'd as soon I didn't."

"Well, that would have been Ed Gelbart's wish," said Crouse. "Nothing to be revealed, even hinted at, before the reading of the will."

"Old feller liked surprisin' folks?" asked Stretch.

To that, Crouse fervently replied, "He was an uncomplicated old gentleman. I might say predictable — but not all the time."

The distance between Lone Star's south quarter and the ranch headquarters was considerable. It was 9.45 when they first sighted the great hacienda and the adobe bunkhouses and network of corrals, but 10.05 before they reached the near edge of the broad front yard. Duff Wheatley was on hand, also a couple of hands. He instructed them to cool and water the buggy horse and the trouble-shooters' mounts.

Crouse climbed down and began introducing the tall men.

"Save your breath, son, I'd know 'em anywheres," drawled Duff. He offered a gnarled paw and an affable grin. "I'm Duff Wheatley, ramrod here. Real pleasure meetin' you tumbleweeds."

"Likewise, Duff," Larry responded as they shook hands. "Which part of Texas you from?"

"Same part as you bucks," said Duff.

"Panhandle. Ed and me both. Ain't never been back. How about you? You get homesick?"

"We went back a while back," Stretch told him. "Didn't linger all that long. Damned if we didn't get into a scrap, a big'un."

"Cavalry post called Fort Mitchum," offered Larry. "Comancheros came a'raidin', so we had to help fight 'em off."

"Oughtn't've fazed you none," shrugged Duff. "Fightin' all the time, ain't you?"

"It gets irksome, Duff," grouched Stretch.

"We'd better get on to the house," urged Crouse. The foreman accompanied them to the front porch. Plump Carmen Bedoya admitted them, obviously impressed by the strangers' generous height. Larry greeted her in her native tongue.

"Buenos dias, Señora."

"Me alegro de conocerle," she responded with a smile. "This way, señors, por favor."

If she was impressed by the tall men, they were awestruck, feeling like fishes out of water in such luxurious surroundings. As they followed the housekeeper along a thick-carpeted hall, Crouse quietly remarked to them that the late Sadie Gelbart was responsible for the home's interior decoration and furnishing.

"She was a lady of excellent taste."

They entered the spacious parlor in which there was ample seating. Already assembled were the Sherwoods, Jesse and his wife, Vern and the other Bedoyas. At first, the newcomers had eyes only for the fine portrait in pride of place on the rear wall. Then, while Crouse introduced them, they shifted their gaze and held battered Stetsons to chests.

"Mister and Mrs Morton Sherwood, Mister and Mrs Jesse Gelbart — you've already met Mister Vernon Gelbart . . . "

"No aches or pains, gentlemen?" Vern asked genially.

"We feel fine, thanks," muttered Stretch. "A mite mixed up on account of we don't savvy why we're here, but fine."

"Which of these persons is the beneficiary you couldn't name, may I enquire?" challenged Elva.

"Mister Lawrence Valentine, ma'am," said Crouse, indicating Larry. "And the other gentleman is his good friend Mister Woodville Emerson."

"Why is *he* here?" she demanded, her disdainful eyes fixing on the taller drifter.

"They come as a pair, Elva," Jesse said with a wry grin.

"They are inseparable, Mrs Sherwood," said Crouse. "Your father was aware of that. He would not have protested Mister Emerson's presence."

"Then *we* shouldn't," insisted Vern.

"I'm certainly not objecting," said Jesse.

Mort Sherwood made a ceremony of consulting his watch and eyeing the lawyer accusingly.

"You are late," he complained. "Thirteen minutes late."

"You superstitious, mister?" Duff mildly enquired while seating himself.

"It is business courtesy for a lawyer to be on time," declared Mort.

"My apologies, Mister Sherwood," said Crouse.

"Well, shucks now," shrugged Duff. "If you got your mind set on gripin' about it, you can blame me. These boys're Texan like me. Texans get together, they chew the fat some."

Proud of his status of foreman-cum-family retainer, he could not be fazed by the pomposity of any big shot from the California capital, and did not hesitate to show it. Mort flushed angrily and took a seat; so did Carmen, the lawyer and the drifters.

Crouse unfastened his satchel and produced the will. As he tore the flap of the envelope and withdrew the document, he began his preamble.

"All concerned parties being present, it is now my duty to read to you the last will and testament of the esteemed Edward Jesse Gelbart, my client and friend."

"Kindly dispense with these preliminaries and come to the point, announce the bequests," ordered Elva.

"Patience, Sis," appealed Vern.

"Don't call me Sis," she snapped.

"Time is money," grouched her husband, checking his watch again. "Just get on with it, all right?"

"As you wish, Mister Sherwood," shrugged Crouse, unfolding the will. "Beneficiaries are listed as follows. To my foreman, friend and confidant of more years than either of us could recall, Duff Wheatley, I bequeath the sum of thirty thousand dollars . . . "

"Doggone," interjected Duff. "He didn't have to do that. Ten'd be plenty. Five would've been fine."

"There's a stipulation that you continue to serve as foreman of Lone Star for as long as you so desire," Crouse told him. "In simple terms, Duff, you can never be fired."

He cleared his throat. "I'll resume. My loyal servants and friends, Mateo and Carmen Bedoya, are to each receive the sum of thirty thousand dollars." Carmen's eyes filled; she held a handkerchief to her eyes while her husband crossed himself. "The sum of thirty thousand dollars is bequeathed to their daughters, Rosa and Juanita, to be held in trust for them until they come of age."

The Bedoya girls traded wondering looks. Elva addressed them sternly.

"I hope you girls — and your parents — are duly appreciative of my father's generosity."

"Come on, Elva, it's the least they deserve," frowned Jesse. "Carmen and Mateo helped raise us, Duff too."

"May we proceed?" Elva hissed at Crouse.

"By all means," he nodded. "To my only daughter, Elva Gelbart Sherwood, I bequeath . . ."

"Now we're getting to it," grinned Mort.

116

" . . . the sum of one hundred thousand dollars," read Crouse.

Elva's eyebrows shot up.

"Mister Crouse, did you read that correctly?"

"Only a hundred thousand?" blustered Mort. "The old man was a millionaire — plus,"

"No mistake, Mrs Sherwood," Crouse said calmly. "If I may proceed? To my son, Jesse, I bequeath the sum of one hundred thousand dollars." No comment from Jesse. "To my son Vernon, I bequeath the sum of one hundred thousand dollars."

"That'll do it," Vern said cheerfully. "I'm about to become an actor-producer."

"Weren't you listening?" gasped his sister. "It's a pittance! Consider the size of our father's fortune, his land holding, his . . . !"

"A hundred thousand — is a *pittance*?" Trudy asked dazedly.

"How could *you* understand?" snorted Elva. "You with your humble origins."

"Humble but a hundred percent respectable, Elva." Jesse stared hard at her. "Listen, we'll get along as brother and sister should, as our parents always wanted, but not if you keep talking down to my wife."

"Now just a minute . . . " began Mort.

"I'm talking to my sister," growled Jesse. Crouse was impassive, Duff and the Bedoyas at ease during the exchange that followed, Jesse firmly reminding Elva that, by marriage, Trudy was a Gelbart and rated the respect due all Gelbarts, Vern tactfully suggesting Mort should refrain from comment. As for the Texans, they were wishing they were out of earshot of this family quarrel; out by a bunkhouse would be fine, socializing with hired hands, their own kind.

While the wrangling continued, the lawyer took the opportunity to fill and light his pipe. The sound of the match flaring distracted Elva in mid-sentence.

118

"That can't be all!" she complained.

"Of course not," said Crouse, "There's more. I just didn't want to interrupt."

"I'll apologize for all of us, Mister Crouse," said Jesse. "And I'll be first to say you're showing us considerable more courtesy than you've received."

"Quite all right," Crouse assured him, and quoted the final bequest. "Having felt for him a great respect and affection for a period of almost twenty years, all the time regretting we were never to meet, I bequeath to Lawrence Valentine the balance of my estate . . ."

"*What* . . . ?" screamed Elva.

Larry's jaw sagged. Stretch turned and gawked at him. Duff traded knowing grins with the Bedoyas. The brothers frowned at each other. Mort jerked to his feet, bug-eyed and red-faced, noisily protesting, "We don't even know this — this — what is he? A saddle-tramp . . . ?"

"This is an outrage!" wailed Elva. "How could Father do this to us?"

"It's a joke, right?" Larry challenged Crouse. "No joke, Mister Valentine," said Crouse. "As of right now, you own this ranch, the ground it stands on, every acre of Lone Star range and the balance of my client's cash assets in the County Security Bank."

"It's crazy!" shouted Mort.

Larry shouted right back at him.

"How d'you suppose *I* feel? I didn't even *know* Ed Gelbart!"

Vern began an attempt to restore order. "Please!" he begged. "We're over-reacting here. Sis — Elva — you're hamming it up. Let's consider this unexpected turn of events — quietly."

"Keep your theatrical expressions to yourself, Vernon Gelbart!" raged his sister. "How dare Father make fools of us! That Lone Star should be inherited by a stranger is — just too bizarre! It's unthinkable, preposterous . . . !"

"We'll contest the will!" declared Mort. "The old man must've been out of his mind!"

Rallying from his shock, Jesse glowered

120

at his brother-in-law.

"Last warning, Mort. If you ever again question Dad's sanity, you'll return to Sacramento minus your front teeth."

"Jesse!" chided Trudy.

"Could we . . . ?" began Vern.

"Hold your tongue!" ordered Elva.

Crouse leaned back in his chair, puffed at his pipe and studied the ceiling. He, Duff and the Bedoyas were the only parties maintaining their composure. Larry was aghast, Stretch shaking his head dazedly, wondering if he were dreaming. Everybody, the lawyer reflected, was reacting pretty much as he had anticipated; he also conceded the reactions were normal.

Larry won silence by rising. At full volume, his booming baritone dominated; the other people might as well have been whispering.

"Listen up! I want to make one thing clear!" They stared at him. He returned their stares, his angry eyes switching from face to face. "Any jackass calls me a fortune-hunter, he's got a fight on his hands. Only reason I'm here is I was sent for. I didn't know a doggone thing about — any of this. You think *you're* fazed? *I'm* fazed . . . "

"I'm spooked," Stretch said uneasily. "This whole deal — too rich for my blood."

"I can't make a lick of sense of it," declared Larry. He studied the portrait, then glanced at Jesse. "I'm with you, son. Ain't callin' your pa loco, but it's for sure he was . . . "

"A touch whimsical — I think that's what you mean," offered Vern. "Don't hate me for saying that, big brother. I'm not denigrating the old man, just stating a fact."

"All right, so that's how he was," continued Larry. "But you folks got to understand I'm as shook up as you. Mad too!"

"Really?" sneered Mort.

"As if *you* have cause for anger," Elva said scathingly.

"You don't know me, never saw

me or my partner till now," Larry pointed out.

"Some of us know you by reputation," muttered Jesse.

"Bueno," growled Larry. "You ever hear of my partner and me hankerin' to get rich and settle down? We never *could* settle."

"That's why we drift," explained Stretch.

"So," Larry told the Sherwoods, "if you think this is what we want, you got another think comin'."

"Larry," said Crouse. "Please remember you'll be in possession of certain information four days from now. For you to renounce your inheritance at this moment would perhaps be precipitate."

"We'll challenge the will." Elva appealed to her brothers. "We *have* to — you must agree. Dear heaven, our birthright is at stake!"

"We're family, we have to contest the will," Jesse nodded. "But I believe Larry. He's as confused as we are, so I for one bear him no animosity."

"Exactly how I feel," said Vern.

"I should mention, now that you've decided to contest the will . . ." began Crouse.

"I'll wire my attorney in Sacramento today," announced Mort. "And draft a letter instructing him accordingly."

"You'll require a copy of the will, which I'll be glad to supply," said Crouse. "However, it's my duty to emphasize that until some court action begins, Mister Valentine is in charge of Lone Star and entitled to reside here with his friend. At this stage, no member of the family has a legal right to order him to leave."

"I refuse to live under the same roof as these common trail-tramps," sniffed Eva. "The very idea! Sharing our home with strangers . . ."

"Ain't strangers, Elva child," drawled Duff. "Well, not to your pa and me. Like it says in Ed's will, he was plumb disappointed he never met 'em, but he didn't think of 'em as strangers."

"You needn't fret, ma'am," Larry

grimly assured Elva. "We don't roost where we ain't wanted." He made a snap decision then, and only because the overt hostility of the Sherwoods had aroused his ire; who the hell did they think they were? "If the old man wanted for us to bunk here, that's what we'll do, but not here in the house." He glanced at Duff. "Any free space for us in some bunkhouse?"

"Well now — Boss," said the foreman. "I don't reckon Ed'd want you bunkin' with the hired hands. We can do better'n that. There's a cosy adobe along from the barn oughta suit you boys just fine. Two beds, a parlor, and your own bathroom with an inside pump."

"Much obliged, amigo," nodded Larry. "We'll settle for that." Now he stared hard at Elva and her husband. "But we'll eat right here in the ranch-house."

"Sounds just right to me," decided Stretch. "We're partial to woman-cookin'."

"And I'll bet you dish up elegant chow," Larry genially remarked to Carmen, who acknowledged the compliment with an eager smile.

"This will be intolerable," complained Elva. "We Gelbarts forced to take our meals with . . . "

"With the likes of us?" challenged Larry. "Don't worry about it, ma'am. We don't eat with our hands."

"'Scuse me, ma'am," frowned Stretch. "But we handle a knife and fork as roper as any other folks."

"Moving into separate quarters is your own decision," said Jesse. "I'd like it understood Trudy and I don't share my sister's aversion to your sharing the old home with us."

"Nor do I," declared Vern.

"*Some* of us have standards," Mort said curtly, then snapped a question at the lawyer. "Anything else in the will we ought to know about?"

"Just the routine proviso," shrugged Crouse. "In the event of Mister Valentine's demise, your wife and her brothers become joint owners of Lone Star, each sharing a third of all assets."

"Don't even think of it, Mister Sherwood suh." Duff could not resist saying it. "You got a snow-flake's chance in hell of shootin' Larry when he ain't lookin'. Better men than you've tried it and bought 'emselves a whole mess of grief."

"That isn't funny," scowled Mort.

"Sure, bad joke," agreed Duff, feigning extreme contrition. "'Scuse me if I don't beg your pardon on bended knees. I'm a mite rheumaticky nowadays."

"By your leave, ladies and gentlemen," Crouse rose to leave. "I have to get back to town now."

After the lawyer walked out, the Texans got to their feet. Larry nodded affably to Jesse, his wife and brother and calmly remarked to the Sherwoods, "We'll see you folks lunchtime."

Duff followed them out, waving to Crouse, who now drove off. As he began conducting them toward the barn, Stretch said, "Hell, Duff."

"Uh huh," grunted the ramrod. "You fiddlefoots're plumb fazed. I reckon Ed figured you'd be."

"You got any notion why he . . . ?" began Larry.

"Don't ask," chided Duff. "Him and me were saddlepards a long time. One thing he admired about me is I'm no blabbermouth."

"Why me?" fretted Larry.

"I swear," sighed Stretch. "You and me, runt, we've wandered far and some powerful peculiar things've happened to us, but this beats all."

"Ain't *that* the truth," grouched Larry.

They had passed the barn when the younger Bedoya girl overtook them, toting a paper-wrapped bundle. As she offered it to Larry, she explained her father believed their 'patron' would wish him to have it. Larry nodded his thanks, the girl scuttled back to the ranch-house and he hefted the bundle. Before he could put the obvious question to the impassive foreman, that veteran said, "Don't ask. You'll find out for yourself."

"Sure hope you savvy this is a bad time for my ol' buddy, Duff," Stretch muttered as they moved on. "He's a hombre never could abide a mystery and — comes to mysteries — this'un's a doozy."

"Suit you?" asked Duff, gesturing to the building they had reached.

He lounged in the doorway of the adobe, watching them check its appointments. It had everything a couple of perplexed drifters might need at this time. The place was clean, the rugs in good condition, the beds comfortable, the added bathroom functional.

"Better'n a hotel room," was Stretch's comment.

"Hands're tendin' your horses," said Duff. "I'll have one of 'em fetch your gear. Anything else you need, ask anybody, the Bedoyas, me, any of the bunkhouse gang."

"We got more'n we need," Larry said distractedly.

"You'll know when it's eatin' time," said Duff. "Baldy, the chuck-boss, he clangs his triangle. That's when you head for the house. Here at Lone Star, family eats luncheon and supper same time as the hired help. His get breakfast at sunup, family around quarter to eight. You got any questions?"

"Hundreds," said Larry. "But you ain't gonna answer 'em."

"So *I* got a question," said Duff. "Orders? You're boss now. Whatever you want done, you tell me, it gets done."

"C'mon, Duff," chided Larry. "Quit joshin' me."

"Who's joshin'?" drawled Duff. "You done inherited this spread. That makes you boss."

"Duff, we got a passel of years 'tween us and we're both Texans, so I don't want to have to fight you," growled Larry. Duff raised an eyebrow in mild enquiry. "We're gonna fight?"

"If you ever call me Boss," declared Larry.

"Bueno — Larry," nodded Duff. "But I'm still askin'. Any orders?"

"Yeah — and you ought to have guessed," said Larry. "No changes. Everything like it was before old Ed cashed in. The hands do what they always do, tend the herd, hunt strays. *You* do like you've always done."

"You're the boss — Larry," grinned Duff. Before withdrawing from the doorway, he pointed to the bundle Larry had dropped on a bed. "Take a look at that stuff. Too bad you and Ed never did meet — but he sure knew you."

Larry squatted on one bed, Stretch on the other.

They stared at each other.

5

A Degree of Acceptance

FLATLY, Stretch said, "It's plain loco."

"And then some," fretted Larry. "But we got to believe Duff and the lawyer. Old Ed was no fool."

"Had to be a helluva cattleman," opined Stretch. "This spread you own is no two-bit outfit."

"You got to say that?" scowled Larry.

"It's in the will," Stretch reminded him. "You own Lone Star. Mightn't always own it, what with that horse's ass from Sacramento claimin' *his* lawyer can fix everything. But, till that happens, it's all yours."

"We were stuck too long at Gibbsville," muttered Larry. "Now we're gonna be stuck *here*."

"Think you ought to take a look at that?" Stretch nodded to the bundle on Larry's bed. "What's in there?"

Larry felt at it.

"Full of paper, seems like."

He slipped the knot of the frayed string securing the bundle. The wrapping fell away, revealing the contents. Newspaper. Some of it yellowing of age. Not whole editions. Clippings, a great many of them.

"I'll be dogged," breathed Stretch.

"All about us," Larry observed after examining a few pieces. "Cut from papers from all over, some of 'em dated fifteen — hell! — twenty years back."

"Old Ed kept tabs on us, saved all that stuff," frowned Stretch. "Duff said he knew you good. I guess this's what he meant."

He changed position to squat beside his partner. They selected and read reports of their escapades and the memories came flooding back, stories of their clashes with the lawless, outlaws fought and defeated, thieves and killers whose names they'd forgotten long ago.

"That Sabado Creek ruckus — I scarce remember it," mused Larry. "And these other places. Sweeney. Beecher's Ford . . ."

"And here's one about them renegades, the Montoya gang, we tangled with way down south," offered Stretch. "Sonofagun. That was the longest time ago."

"This one's about the Piketown flood — how could we forget that?" sighed Larry.

"Hey, that hullabaloo at New Chance," grinned Stretch. "Town where they tried and hung a killer name of Billy Reese, and newspaper scribblers came from all the big cities . . ."

"The Hammer gang — Black Jack Hammer." Larry discarded a cutting and picked up another. "And the time we bodyguarded the governor of Colorado. And Delarno, Oregon. We near died there, would've if Doc

Beaumont hadn't helped the local doc patch us. All these boss-bandidos, the one called El Capitan, Kane Braddock, Webb's Box W bunch — so many of 'em."

Ed Gelbart's collection of cuttings jogged their memories. They should have felt older, especially when forced to recall crises dating back seventeen years and earlier. Should have felt older, but didn't.

What they did feel was nostalgia, gratitude and not a little incredulity. How could this be? How could two tumbleweeds become embroiled in one baffle after another, outwit and outfight so many desperadoes for so many years — and survive? Not that they always survived unscathed. They had been wounded time and time again; death had been close on innumerable occasions and they had ample reminders, scars aplenty and the now and again twinge of pain in an arm or a leg or a shoulder. Lady Luck had been with them, but the Grim Reaper was hanging around more often than not.

Fervently, Stretch muttered an understatement.

"I guess — uh — we've been kind of busy."

"Damn right," agreed Larry.

"The old feller liked what we did," Stretch realized. "Must've liked us too. I mean — savin' all this stuff."

"Texan, our kind of man," reflected Larry. "We'd have liked him."

"Oh, sure," nodded Stretch. "Him and us'd talk up a storm, drink good sourmash and hit it off like old amigos from way back — but does that make it sense for him to blame well sign his whole spread over to you?"

"Makes no sense at all," complained Larry. "but he did it and, like everybody keeps tellin' me, he wasn't loco." He dug out his Durham sack and began building a smoke, his brow creased in deep thought. "That letter he left for me, the one I got to wait four days for, I wish I had it right now."

"Might explain a few things, you think?" prodded Stretch.

"Well, one thing's for sure," declared Larry. "*Somebody* better explain. And, even though he's dead, it's up to him."

"For four days, you're gonna be miserable company for me," Stretch predicted. "Jumpy as a turkey a couple days before Thanksgivin'."

"No I won't," growled Larry. "Already decided I'm gonna play it cool. Let Elva and her man act uppity. I don't care a damn. Duff's friendly, them Bedoyas keep smilin' at us and I don't reckon we'll tangle with the brothers or that gentle little Trudy. I figure I can stay patient for four days."

They had a visitor. Vern came to the doorway, looked in and, with a grin, said, "Permission to enter the quarters of the new owner of Lone Star?"

"I wish your sister was a joker, Vern," said Larry. "C'mon in and set."

Vern helped himself to a chair and studied them.

137

"Thanks to the Fourth Estate, I already knew you by reputation," he remarked. "Jesse has told me more. My sister? Overplays the class-consciousness, sees herself as a woman of distinction, but she's a good soul at heart. Well, quite a situation we have here. It'll take you a little time to get used to the idea I imagine."

"Vern, Larry ain't *never* gonna get used to it," said Stretch. "Me neither."

"Don't take this personally," begged Vern. "This is only temporary. I'm no expert in legal procedure but, in a case of this kind, the court invariably rules in favor of the parties contesting the will. The next of kin are considered the rightful heirs, especially when an estate is bequeathed to a person the deceased has never even met. As a member of the family, I feel bound to support Elva's challenge, as Jesse does." He eyed them cautiously. "I hope I'm not offending. I certainly don't mean to."

"Hey, I *like* what you're sayin', boy," Larry assured him. "It means we ain't gonna be stuck here."

"You'll have to restrain your nomadic instincts a while longer I'm afraid," said Vern. "Don't count on leaving in a couple of weeks. These things take time. It could be months before the court gives its ruling."

"Aw, hell," grumbled Stretch.

Larry got around to lighting his cigarette, studying Vern the while.

"You ain't as riled up as your sister about this thing," he observed.

"Well, it's not as though the old man cut us off without a penny," replied Vern. "A hundred thousand isn't chicken-feed, is it? For an actor with aspirations to becoming a producer and furthering his career, it's a windfall. Frankly, I'm more amused than disgruntled by my father's quirky behaviour. One of his most endearing characteristics was his sense of humor. My mother, God rest her soul, appreciated it. So did Jesse and me."

"But not sister Elva?" prodded Larry.

Vern shrugged helplessly.

"Sometimes I wonder how she could become so — I'll use a term with which you're bound to be familiar — high-falutin'. She didn't inherit it from either of our parents."

"Folks get hitched and beget young'uns," Stretch philosophized. "And sometimes the kids ain't all alike. I got three sisters and they ain't nothin' like me. Had a kid brother died of typhoid when I was around nine and he was shapin' up to bein' a whole lot different from me."

"We Gelbarts are quite a mix," reflected Vern. "I think Jesse and I must've been a disappointment to our father, neither of us following in his footsteps. Jesse was always good with figures, so I suppose it was inevitable he's become an accountant. And my urge to be a man of the theatre — Dad could never have foreseen that."

"It's nice you and Jesse ain't against us, Vern," said Larry. "Seems the joke's on us as much as you Gelbarts.

We ain't the kind to settle in and boss a big cattle spread."

"We're just drifters," declared Stretch.

"And your pa knew that," frowned Larry.

"May I?" Vern rose, moved to Larry's bed and briefly inspected the clippings. "Great day in the morning! Collecting and studying this information year after year, could there be anything he *didn't* know about you?" He turned, retreated to the door and, before leaving, remarked wistfully, "That was typical of him. Another admirer of yours, relishing newspaper accounts of your adventures, might have pasted them in a scrapbook. But not old Ed. He just wrapped them in brown paper and hoarded them like a beaver. See you at lunch."

Lunch would have been an awkward meal for the Texans had Elva and her husband been allowed to dominate the conversation. Disapproval was not the word for their attitude toward the tall men; contempt was what they were

141

showing. They assembled in the most grand furnished dining-room either drifter had seen in a month of Sundays. Elva seated herself at one end of the table. Carmen stood by the chair at the head of the table and nodded to Larry, indicating this was his rightful place.

"That's where the patron always sat, señora," he guessed.

"Si," she smiled. "Siempre."

"Gracias," he nodded. The others were watching him. He looked at Jesse. "You bein' the firstborn son, I'd feel easier if you used his chair."

"I call that thoughtful," Jesse acknowledged. "Mighty thoughtful."

"Seems fittin'," said Larry.

He and Stretch waited till the others were seated before choosing places.

"Just as well you two know your place," was Mort's first jibe.

"Always have known, Mister Sherwood," Larry replied while Carmen and her daughters served the first course.

"On account of we're used to it," offered Stretch.

"The wide open spaces," Vern said knowingly.

"One acknowledges certain Indian tribes to be nomadic, said Elva, "Not white men."

"Wrong, Elva," countered Jesse. "You have a short memory. Vern, you remember Zeke and Elroy?"

"Who could forget those old fiddle-foots?" grinned Vern. For the benefit of his sister-in-law and the Texans, he recalled, "They used to show up same time every year, just before spring roundup and, as cowhands say, work their butts off."

"A disgusting expression," sniffed Elva.

"Top hands they were," said Jesse.

"Not just expert herders," enthused Vern. "Any horses needed breaking, Zeke and Elroy would get the job done, and with great efficiency. For good measure, they'd cut shingles, handle repairs around the place, attack any chore Dad or Duff assigned them. After round-up, they'd collect their pay and return to their wandering — until the same time the next year."

"The wanderlust," Trudy commented.

"Right, honey," nodded Jesse. "And they were only two of many. Always another river to be crossed, another mountain to be climbed." He grinned at the Texans. "A way of life, you'd say?"

"That's what it is, sure," agreed Larry.

"I've sent a courier into Hart City . . . " Mort stopped eating to make an announcement, "with a telegram to be sent to a legal firm in Sacramento, also a letter to be mailed with a copy of the will enclosed and full instructions."

"Bueno," approved Stretch.

"Little sister, some wanderers achieve fame," declared Vern. "Our tall friends . . . "

"They are hardly that," Elva protested. "Friends, indeed."

" . . . have become celebrities," continued Vern. "On more than one occasion, they have acted as bodyguards to European royalty visiting our frontier territories."

"Really?" Trudy asked eagerly.

"We just happened to be around when they needed a little help," Larry told her.

"And how many drifters can claim to be personally acquainted with the Vice-President of these United States?" challenged Vern.

"Vice-President Jordan Barclay himself?" exclaimed Trudy.

"I refuse to believe . . . " began Elva.

"You have to," said Jesse. "It was big news at the time."

"In all the papers, Sis," said Vern.

"An assassination attempt," recalled Jesse. "The crisis came to a head in — was it Colorado, Larry?"

"Colorado — I think," said Larry.

"So there you are," Vern said cheerfully. "But for the intervention of Larry and Stretch, a vice president would have been gunned down by killers hired by men in high places."

"What is he like?" Trudy wanted to know. "Friendly, ma'am," said Larry.

"Right likeable hombre," recalled Stretch. "Well, that's how it goes. Folks're folks. Some're rich or important, some ain't. But scratch 'em and they all bleed the same color blood."

Elva wasn't through yet.

"Why should our father have admired these men?" she demanded. "He was a man of great wealth and social standing. No matter how impressive their adventures may seem, they are vagabonds."

"They're Texan," said Jesse. "So was Dad."

"I'm a businessman and practical," growled Mort. "Valentine, you'd be a fool to believe you could retain ownership of this property. When my lawyers get to work . . .

"I try real hard to never be a fool," Larry assured him. "Still and all, nobody's perfect."

"Somethin' you don't seem to savvy,

146

mister," Stretch told Mort. "My partner's kind of stubborn."

"But there can be no doubt as to the outcome of this legal action against you," blustered Mort.

"No doubt whatsoever," insisted Elva.

"I guess not," shrugged Larry.

"So why not leave at once?" demanded Mort.

"Now, Mort . . . " began Jesse.

"It's okay, Jesse," said Larry, glancing at Mort. "We'll be leavin' — when we're good and ready."

"It's this away, mister," offered Stretch. "You got a big surprise when the lawyer read the will, but so did Larry. He don't savvy why Mister Gelbart did what he did, and he's always leery of what he don't savvy. Got to find an answer for everythin', my ol' buddy."

"If that ain't clear enough for you, my partner'd be glad to explain it all again," Larry told Mort.

Mort turned red. Trudy fought hard

to suppress a chuckle while her brother-in-law, stage trained and never stuck for words, reminded his relatives,

"There'll be other shock reactions all over the county. Lone Star will become even more famous."

"We want no publicity!" protested Elva.

"Can't be avoided," shrugged Vern. "After formal reading of any will, its contents cease to be privileged information. Unless of course there is a proviso that the information be kept secret. And our father made no such stipulation, dear sister."

"I can't bear this!" cried Elva. "The lawyer is at liberty to . . . ?"

"To satisfy the curiosity of the Press — in the person of the editor of the local paper," smiled Vern. "Like it or not, there'll be publicity. Joe Mirram, I'm sure, will publish a special edition. Only to be expected, you know. It's not every day that a wandering outlaw-fighter inherits a cattle empire."

"The whole county will know!" she

wailed. "I won't be able to show my face in town!"

"You think people'll feel sorry for us?" Jesse dryly challenged. "We three who were left only a hundred thousand dollars each?"

"A hundred thousand dollars," Trudy repeated dazedly. "So *much* money."

Larry was glad when the meal ended, Stretch even more so. On the porch, they retrieved their sidearms and strapped them on. Duff was straddling the toprail of a corral. They quit the porch, crossed the broad yard diagonally and, reaching the corral, climbed up to join the ramrod and build and light their after lunch smokes. Jesse emerged from the house, donned his Stetson and decided to join them.

"Forgot to fetch a cigar," he remarked, swinging up to perch beside them.

Larry said, while offering Bull Durham, "I guess you still know how."

"I still know how, Larry." Jesse nodded his thanks and began rolling a quirley. "I was raised here, and that's something I'll always be grateful for."

Stretch gave him a light. They smoked and talked a while, Duff joining in, but in his own taciturn way, blocking Larry's every effort to draw him out. Nonchalantly, he agreed he had enjoyed his old companero's confidence.

"Wasn't much Ed kept from me."

"The will was no surprise to you?" prodded Jesse.

"Well now, a lotta things surprise me," drawled Duff. "It's just nobody can tell from lookin' at me."

"One thought occurred to me, but I dismissed it," said Jesse. "For just a moment, I wondered if this was Dad's way of punishing us."

"You oughta know better, son," chided Duff.

"I do know better," Jesse said emphatically. "That's why I shook the thought off. He wasn't a man to harbor resentments. Whatever his reason for leaving the ranch to Larry, it wasn't

150

to punish his daughter and sons. Hell, if punishment was his motive, he'd have left us nothing. No, there was no spite in him, no meanness — even though — I suppose we were a disappointment to him."

"Would he be all that sorry, the way you three turned out?" asked Stretch.

"Ain't as if you and Vern're no-accounts," remarked Larry.

"We're a success in our chosen fields," said Jesse. "Vern must be an above-average actor, must be, because there are so many demands for his services. Elva married well. As for me, I think Dad felt I was still connected with the cattle business, and that was some consolation to him."

"Boy, if that outfit you work for was shippin' fish or timber, he'd've been plumb disgusted." Duff grinned mildly. "Yup, I recall he said somethin' like 'At least Cullen and Drew're packin' and shippin' beef.' Don't reckon he was mad at you."

After a brief silence, Larry put a

question to Jesse, "Could *you* run this spread?"

"Certainly could," said Jesse. "Just by following Dad's routine, and especially with Duff still foreman of Lone Star. I'd keep it going the way it's always operated. But it's too early to think of it. By the terms of the will, you're the new owner here. I've no doubt the court will turn everything around and rule the old man's kin are rightful heirs to Lone Star. But, until then, and these things take time, you're the boss and I for one won't dispute any decisions you make."

"Larry ain't changin' nothin'," declared Duff. "Already said it, and he's the kind stands by what he says."

"That's how it's gonna be, Jesse," said Larry. Another brief silence, then, "'Scuse me for askin', if it's none of my business," said Stretch. "That purty little wife of yours, she feelin' poorly?"

"Was," said Jesse. "But she keeps

improving. From the day we arrived here, she began feeling better. It's healthier for her here, Stretch. We're a long way from San Francisco, the dampness, the fog."

Larry was irritated by Duff's reticence but, at the same time, respected him. He was convinced the ramrod knew more than he was prepared to tell, and obviously because his old compadre had demanded he stay close-mouthed. So be it. He had to admire Duff for that. And keep a tight rein on his patience.

Later, he complained to his partner, "Four days from now is startin' to feel like four years from now."

"Sure," Stretch sympathized. "But you can hold out, runt."

"Got no choice," shrugged Larry.

"Betcha life it'll all be in Ed's letter, everything you're wonderin' and frettin' about," soothed Stretch. "Meantime, we're comfortable enough here, good chow, good company."

"'Cept for . . ." began Larry.

"Uh huh," nodded Stretch. "Ornery Elva and her unsociable man."

★ ★ ★

It was 2 p.m. of that day when Gordon Crouse stopped by the *Journal* to put the editor out of his misery; from the moment he'd sighted the lawyer quitting town with the Texans, Joe Mirram had seethed with curiosity, his newsman's instincts playing hell with his digestion. There would be something unusual about the Gelbart will, something special. This was his hunch, but never in his wildest dreams would he have anticipated what Crouse had to tell him.

"Valentine?" His mouth opened wide; his half-smoked cigar slid from his mouth to his desk to be hastily retrieved. "He inherits the whole shebang? *Valentine?*"

"You aren't listening," grinned Crouse. "Each of old Ed's children will be a hundred thousand dollars richer."

154

"Yeah, I heard you." Mirram nodded excitedly. "But Valentine — full owner of the biggest ranch in . . . ?"

"It can only be temporary, Joe," said Crouse. "The Sherwoods will contest the will and Jesse and Vern, being family, will follow their sister's lead."

"This much I know about the law," muttered Mirram. "That kind of legal mumbo-jumbo takes *time*."

"It does," agreed Crouse. "And there can be no doubt of the outcome. But, meanwhile, Larry Valentine is officially boss of Lone Star."

"I don't care if those tearaways come down on me like a bolt of lightning!" gasped Mirram. "This story — hell — it's unique! Never in a million years could I pass it up! It rates a special edition!"

"You're reacting exactly as I expected." Crouse was chuckling now.

"Valentine and his partner are publicity-shy, but I have to risk their anger," said Mirram. "Damn, it, they have to understand. This is *big* news!

"They can be reasonable I'm sure," said Crouse. "Sometimes, fatalists are the most reasonable people one could meet, and there can be no denying they *are* fatalists."

By mid-morning of the morrow, the special edition was circulating throughout Hart City and county-wide. Mirram had unearthed his copy of a photograph of the notorious trouble-shooters taken many years before. The picture was right there on the front page under the banner headline.

After reading the report, Mayor Burford assured the county treasurer, "I don't think I'll get overheated about this, but Holly and George don't like surprises. It'd be just like them to start worrying — needlessly."

"Your calming influence," suggested Kimmer.

"Exactly," grinned Burford. "I'd better treat them to lunch in my suite at the hotel. Get word to them, Otto. Better invite Will too."

Around 12.30 p.m., lunching with

the mayor in his suite at the hotel that bore his name, the saloon-owners and the sheriff were at first uneasy. The Chestnut Saloon's proprietor, George Markey, was a bulky redhead, as dapper as the owner of the Lucky Deal, but not as fat; no man in Hart County was as fat as Holly Orban.

"It's their reputation bothers me," Markey said uneasily.

"Valentine's the dangerous one," complained Apley. "Hell, Moss, he's a snooper from way back and too smart for my likin'."

"Has the instincts of a detective," muttered Kimmer. "I've heard he refused an offer to join the Pinkerton Agency."

"That bastard and his scrawny partner left their mark on my place," scowled Orban. "I had to let Clint go. And my other dealers are still hurting."

Bitter memories of last night's fracas did not affect his appetite; he was as usual gorging himself.

"If you boys'll stop fretting a moment

and listen to the voice of reason . . . "
Burford dabbed at his mouth with a
napkin and showed them a confident
grin, "I'll set your minds at ease."

"Yeah, all right, you're the voice of
reason," Orban conceded. "Go ahead.
Talk to us."

"It's an old man's joke, his way
of having the last laugh," grinned
Burford. "We remember Ed Gelbart
as a good-humored old fellow, right?
Does anybody believe he meant to
deprive his own flesh and blood of
their birthright? He'd never do that.
He *knew* his daughter and sons would
contest the will, knew any challenge
they filed would win. But, meanwhile,
Valentine and his partner are living soft
and easy at Lone Star. I give them six
or seven weeks at most. And, while
they're here, there's no way Valentine'll
become a town councilman."

"If he did, he'd side with Trant and
Doble I bet," frowned Markey.

"It won't happen," said Burford.
"Those drifters will be long gone from

this territory before the next elections.

"You telling us it's business as usual for us?" muttered Orban.

"Why not?" countered Burford. "Even if Valentine found time to get curious about us, what could he do — what could he prove?"

"We're well regulated," Kimmer reminded everybody. "Ours is a carefully organized operation with every eventuality provided for. That's my specialty. All accounts are in order, and available for audit at the prescribed times."

"Know what impregnable means, Holly?" challenged Burford. "That's what we are. Impregnable. We have the perfect set-up and, month by month, we get richer."

"How about those soreheads, Trant and Doble?" demanded Apley.

"They're soreheads, possible they're suspicious, but they're no threat," said Burford. "Will they protest the tax rises? That's hardly likely because, as far as they know, all of us are paying the extra tax. We aren't but there's no way they can prove it. Otto takes care of the books. True, Doble's a money-man and, as a member of the council, entitled to demand he be allowed do a personal audit. What if he did? Otto would supply the right book. Doble would fine tooth comb it and find no irregularities."

"And — uh — old Ed willing his spread to Valentine, we don't have to fret about that?" prodded Markey.

"Neither do the Gelbarts," Burford assured him. "Let's not forget those Texans are restless spirits. Out at Lone Star, they're living in luxury. Some saddletramps would, in their position, count themselves lucky. But not Valentine and Emerson. They'll be *grateful* when the Gelbarts' lawyers win their case. Unless they're stupid, they've already realized they don't have to stay here forever. So, as soon as the court rules in favor of the rightful heirs, they'll ride out of Hart County — probably at a gallop."

Convinced Burford's assessment of

the situation made sense, his cronies relaxed, while two other councilmen discussed the big news in private.

The County Security, established and managed by Abner Doble, was Hart City's only independent bank; the others were branches of the First National, Southwestern and Pioneer Trust companies. Being a prudent man, Doble had insured the County and its cash assets years ago, the same week he first opened for business.

The banks had closed for lunch, and, today, Dave Trant wasn't eating with his family. He and Doble were in conference in a private dining-room of an uptown restaurant. And, predictably, the subject under discussion was the full-of-surprises last will and testament of the late Ed Gelbart.

"Anybody else but Ed, I'd suppose age had affected his mind," said the storekeeper. "But we got Doc's word."

"Yes," nodded Doble. "And we both knew Ed. Lew Richmond has to be right, Dave. Ed was as sane as either of us when he had Gordy Crouse draw up that will. No matter how eccentric it may seem, we can be sure Ed had his reasons."

"Elva and his boys maybe?" suggested Trant. "They left Lone Star to live their own lives, he accepted that, but felt everything had been too easy for them, so decided they'd have to go to court, put up a fight for their shares of his estate?"

"That seems a possibility," agreed Doble. "We remember him as a wily character. Lovable, certainly, but shrewd."

"I guess we know how *he'd* have felt about the latest tax rise," mused Trant.

"He'd be as disgusted as we are," opined Doble. "But he'd have been discreet, keeping his reaction to himself. Another of his qualities, Dave. Discretion."

"Most county folk'll remember him as a rough old cattleman who built his fortune the hard way," Trant supposed. "Everybody knew him."

"But . . . ?" challenged Doble.

"Not everybody understood him," muttered Trant. "I'd say just a handful of us realized he was the smartest citizen of Hart County."

"A keener intelligence than anybody suspected," reflected Doble.

"Just a handful of us, Ab," said Trant. "You, me, Duff Wheatley for sure, Doc and maybe his own sons. I'm not sure."

"Jesse perhaps," said Doble. "Not that young Vern didn't love and respect his father, but Jesse is the one who most reminds me of the old man."

"Ever noticed, after a good friend dies, you find yourself remembering things he said?" asked Trant.

"We all do that," nodded Doble. "It's natural I think."

"He said it to me," Trant confided. "I'm harking back to the night he retired from the council. It was right after the meeting. You'll recall the reason he gave for quitting."

"Pressure of business," said Doble.

163

"A ranch so big made heavy demands on his time."

"He spoke privately to me, Ab." The storekeeper confided softly. "He knew how I felt about Burford and the others. All he said was, 'Stop your fretting, Dave. They'll get theirs, all in good time.' His exact words, Ab."

Doble's reaction was a pensive nod. "Interesting," he remarked. "We should cling to our hopes, my friend. There may still be a chance for us."

6

The Real Legacy

OVER the next few days, the Texans relaxed at Lone Star, one of them anyway. Stretch could find common ground with everybody, all the ranch folk, the obvious exception being the Sherwoods. Though just as gregarious, Larry was on edge, counting the hours before confronting Gordon Crouse again; his benefactor — he hoped — had done him the kindness of leaving some explanation for his outlandish action.

It would be in the letter, he kept assuring himself.

Four days after the reading of the will, the tall men rode into Hart City. They had left Lone Star early, so arrived before 10 a.m. Straight to the photography gallery they rode, there to dismount, tie their horses and climb the steps to Crouse's office.

They knocked and entered, the lawyer rose from his desk to greet them and Larry said in relief, "Time's up, Gordy."

"How're things at Lone Star?" Crouse asked as he moved to his safe. "I imagine, by now, you and Duff are like old friends."

"Gettin' along fine with him and the Gelbart boys," said Larry. "The Bedoyas like us, all the bunkhouse gang too. I think Elva and Mort'd be right pleased if we just up and died."

The lawyer unlocked and opened his safe, took out the envelope and placed it on his desk.

"Take it away if you wish," he offered. "Or maybe you'd prefer to read it right here. You'd have privacy. You're welcome to my office. I'm going home for a while. Doc Richmond's giving Adeline another checkover this morning. I like to be on hand when . . . "

"Yeah, much obliged," nodded Larry.

"Be comfortable," Crouse urged after donning his hat. "Use my chair."

When he had left, Stretch flopped into the chair fronting the desk and rolled and lit a cigarette. Larry planted himself in Crouse's chair, picked up the envelope and studied the inscription.

"From Edward Gelbart to me," he told his partner. "To be read four days after Gordy did his duty out at Lone Star."

"Maybe now you'll learn somethin'," Stretch said encouragingly. "Go on, runt. Get to readin'. And take your time."

Larry tore the flap and extracted and unfolded the sheets of writing paper covered by the cattle baron's surprisingly neat handwriting. There were no misspellings and, to his approval, the old man had ruled against composing the letter in a formal way. It was a long letter and not one word of it would bore him. An understatement. What Ed had chosen to commit to paper started Larry's short hairs tingling.

'Dear Larry,' it read.

'Seems natural for me to use your given name, because from way back when I first read of you and Stretch, I got to thinking of you as my friends. I am putting all this on paper like I am talking to you eyeball to eyeball. Best way, I reckon.

Been cussing me for dumping Lone Star on you? My kids mad at you? They oughtn't be. No way could you be stuck with that big spread forever. Any smart lawyer, any judge, will rule against my will, but all that legal stuff is kind of complicated. So, before you quit Hart County, you and Stretch will have time for what I finagled you here to do. I know you boys cannot settle here nor any other place, but I'm counting on you to oblige an old Texan before your feet start itching.

You have likely guessed how much it grieves me that my sons did not want to be cattlemen like me. But there is no mean streak in Jesse or Vern. Jesse married a good little woman. My girl Elva always was kind of haughty, and I do not know why. Her mother, God rest her soul, never was that way. About Mort, do not let him faze you. He is a horse's ass anyway.

I am going to name men I trust, which means you can trust them too.

Lawyer who drew up my will, Gordy Crouse, is a hundred percent honest. Same goes for my old compadre Duff. You know him by now, so you have pegged him for a straight shooter. Mateo and Carmen and their girls will never give you trouble.

You never did cotton to newspapermen, but you can take my word Joe Mirram is not in cahoots with the big shot thieves of Hart City. Dave Trant, Abner Doble and Doc Richmond deal fair with everybody — else they would not be friends of mine.

Things are not right in Hart City. I respect Abner's savvy. He is smart and careful and, for quite a time, he has been leery of the sharpers now running the town I helped build, a good town. I go along with Abner's suspicions, so next I will name the men you dare *not* trust and had better be wary of.

The mayor, Moss Burford, and councilmen George Markey (Chestnut Saloon) Holly Orban (Lucky Deal Saloon) are switching county funds to their own pockets with plenty help from the County Treasurer, Otto Kimmer. No gambler gets an even break at those saloons. Every tableman on Markey's and Orban's payroll is an expert double-dealer and every game is fixed so the house always wins. We have a crooked sheriff and one of his deputies is just as crooked, meaning Ritchie Neville. Markey and Orban pay them for protection against sore losers.

Doc Richmond says the other deputy, Jay Elhurst, only pretends he is not onto them. Elhurst told Doc he is just biding his time. If Burford is voted out of office, Kimmer, Markey and Orban will

170

go too. Then this territory will have an honest administration and maybe Elhurst will get to be the first honest sheriff since Will Apley was sworn in by Burford.

Those two-timers have been playing it smart. They raise taxes and claim they are making improvements. There have been improvements like at the county school, but Abner claims the cash spent on improvements is nickels and dimes compared to what is collected in taxes.

If I knew how to prove Burford and his lowdown friends are doing what they are doing, I would have taken care of them myself. This is the kind of mess you could clean up like you have done before. Am I asking too much of you and Stretch?

Do it for me, boys. Make Hart City the kind of town it used to be. An honest administration would not tax folks as heavily as Burford and his crooked buddies do. And Hart City's only chance of a square deal is a new administration, which means the sharpers got to be voted out or scared out, and I reckon I can leave that to you.

Always craved to meet you boys. Too bad it never happened. But, though I'll be dead when you read this, you will know it was written by a friend who is counting on you.

Much obliged, amigos.

Ed Gelbart.'

Larry grimaced and decided, this time, he would not try to shuttle a message down to its gist for his partner's benefit. He nudged the three pages across the desk.

"Better you read it too. It'll be easy enough, the way he wrote it all down."

While Stretch read, Larry rose and paced, disgruntled that a wily old Texan had lured him into what would become yet another tense and probably bloody showdown, but also wishing the man were still alive, so he could shake his hand and buy him a shot of good Texas sourmash whiskey.

It took Stretch longer to read the plea, but he comprehended it as clearly as Larry had. He folded it, restored it to the envelope and passed it to Larry, who stowed it' in a pocket. Then he said resignedly, "I guess we're gonna do it. You don't know how, not yet, but we're gonna do it."

"And you know why," growled Larry. "He's dead now. We could burn what he wrote and vamoose from this territory, but could we forget this town and what's happenin' to it — and the folks that live here? Anyway, he was countin' on us, and he was a Texan."

"Well, you'll think of somethin', some way we can start doin' what we got to do," shrugged Stretch. "You just need time, runt."

"I need to parley with one of them hombres Ed said we could trust," frowned Larry. He stopped pacing and perched on a corner of the desk. "One that savvies how tax money's handled.

This Abner Doble'd know but, if I'm seen bendin' his ear, some sonofabitch might get curious." He thought for a moment, then snapped his fingers. "We could talk to Jesse. He savvies all that stuff."

Crouse returned in good humor. In response to Stretch's polite enquiry, he reported that the medico was confident his wife's confinement and delivery would be problem-free. When he resumed his chair, Larry handed him the Gelbart letter and urged-him lock it in his safe again.

"You wish me to keep it for you?"

"Keep it safe," nodded Larry. "Read it if you want. I know you'd never get careless and blab about it — even to them Ed trusted."

Left alone, Crouse did read the plea. He felt a surge of hope when he returned it to his safe and, while the door was open, thoughtfully eyed another envelope. It bore his name, written by the same Ed Gelbart, who had relied on him not to open it until and if a certain change occurred.

He closed and relocked the safe and pocketed the key.

★ ★ ★

The Texans were back at Lone Star in time for lunch. When that meal began, the young- brother talked show business; with part of the $100,000 that would soon be his, he intended producing a play whose author was a close cohort of his. Elva tartly assured him that, soon enough, he would have considerably more than $100,000.

"I've received a reply to my wire," said Mort, eyeing the Texans triumphantly. "Application for our contesting the old man's will has been filed already."

"Bueno," grunted Larry. "I'm real happy for you." Catching Jesse's eye, he asked. "Could we talk some when we're through eatin'? Things I need to know about, stuff I figure you can explain."

"If it's about the running of Lone

Star, Duff could tell you as much as I could, more in fact," offered Jesse.

"No," said Larry. "It's somethin' else."

"Glad to oblige," shrugged Jesse.

"I won't need to rest after lunch," Trudy said cheerily. The Texans had noticed the marked improvement and wondered if she had ever been as healthy as she appeared now; the lady was glowing. "Now that I'm so much stronger, I was going to ask Jesse to take me for a buggy ride across some of Lone Star range."

"I'm sure sorry . . ." began Larry.

"Don't be," she smiled. "I can still enjoy a little tour. Mateo could drive me."

"My cue to voice a better idea," decided Vern. "May *I* volunteer to be your guide? I promise to show you some beautiful scenery and — another promise — not to bore you with accounts of my breaking into show business, my very first audition for a . . ."

"I *insist* you tell me about *that*," she declared.

"Your wish is my command," he grinned. "It had its humorous side, that first audition. I like to hear you laugh, little sister-in-law, so I'll recount it in detail — with gestures if you wish."

"I'll insist on that too," she chuckled.

Assured his wife would enjoy her jaunt with his brother, Jesse was willing to give Larry all the time he needed. They took an after-lunch stroll, he and the trouble-shooters, and Duff Wheatley emerged from the mess-shack while they were making for a low rise beyond the corrals. Spotting the foreman, Larry promptly signalled him to join them.

"He ought to be in on this," he told Jesse.

"In on what?" asked Jesse.

"Give me time," begged Larry. "I'm thinkin' about what questions I'm gonna ask first."

Reaching the rise's grassy summit, the four men squatted cross-legged and smoked. Larry put his first question, aiming it at the weather-beaten ramrod. He had to wait for an answer; Duff couldn't be rushed.

"Well, sure," he drawled at last. "Come payday, Lone Star waddies head for town hankerin' a little pleasure just like every other county cowhand. Saloons get plenty trade paydays."

"The Lucky Deal and the Chestnut," Larry patiently repeated.

"Two places our boys stay clear of," said Duff. "You know why. Got sharped your first night in town, I hear tell. So Lone Star hands're as leery as you. They don't talk it around on accounta it's plain Apley and Neville're in cahoots with Markey and Orban." He added with a knowing grin. "I guess you've read that letter Ed left for you."

"You know what's in that letter?" challenged Larry.

"Just guessin'," shrugged Duff.

"Next question," said Larry, looking at Jesse. "This is just a for instance, you understand."

"A hypothetical question?" asked Jesse. Blank stares from Larry and Stretch. "Sorry. I shouldn't use a word so strange to you. So — for instance?"

"A big town — like Hart City — with what you call an administration," prodded Larry. "How does it run?"

"The town council's in charge," said Jesse. "Usually comprising the elected mayor and various aldermen, leading businessmen for the most part, also a treasurer, the custodian of county funds."

"Tax money."

"Yes."

"So the treasurer's kind of important?"

"Naturally."

"All right, Jesse, supposin' a big piece of that tax money gets sidetracked?"

"Sidetracked?"

"If the councilmen get greedy, start linin' their pockets on the quiet — how could a man prove they're doin' that?"

"The treasurer's duty is to keep records."

"Books?"

"Of course. Ledgers showing the current balance and expenditure."

"And, if the treasurer's coverin' for his buddies, divvyin' up tax money . . . ?"

"An audit would reveal such underhand activities. You're talking about embezzlement, Larry."

"What's a . . . ?"

"An auditor's job is to check the books."

"You savvy all that stuff?"

"I'm chief accountant for C and D. Their books are inspected regularly by auditors."

"Who d'you suppose checks all the accounts here?"

"I'd assume a local man with the necessary experience," frowned Jesse. "Come on now, Larry, why are you asking these questions?"

Larry decided it was time to take Jesse and Duff into his confidence, and did so, repeating Ed Gelbart's suspicions, his naming of certain parties, some trustworthy, some otherwise. During the telling of it, he had the feeling none of it was news to Duff.

Stretch now remarked, "Old Ed was countin' on Larry and me to set things to rights."

"And the best way is for us to get them books," Larry said calmly. "So Jesse can check 'em."

"You can't just demand to inspect the treasurer's records," protested Jesse.

"Where would they keep such stuff?" demanded Larry.

"Big safe," offered Duff. "Kimmer's office, up-stairs at City Hall."

"So," decided Larry, "we're gonna have to bust in there." As Jesse's eyebrows shot up, he thoughtfully added, "After midnight'd be the right time. Wait till the town's closed down and quiet."

"Now just a damn minute!" gasped Jesse.

"Can be done," Duff said mildly, "There's still a few things you didn't know about your pa, boy. Once in a while, he'd hire some hombre that'd been in trouble with the law elsewhere, some thief fresh outa jail and hankerin' to start clean."

"He did that?" blinked Jesse.

"Like I said, just once in a while, and never was one let him down," nodded Duff. "We got a wrangler, Cranney. Damn good man. I'd trust him with my life. Near got himself lynched for horse stealin' 'bout fifteen years back. Old Max, our chuck-boss, did five years in a territorial calaboose for tryin' to hold up a store in some North Utah town. And then there's McGinty. Uh huh, I figure he could get us into City Hall, open that safe for us too. It's been a long time. He'd be a mite rusty, and he'll be some surprised when I tell him how he's gonna help us, but he'll do it. He sure had respect for Ed."

"Look, Jesse, if this idea spooks you, that's okay, you don't have to come along," soothed Larry. "We'll fetch the books back here and you can take your time lookin' 'em over."

Jesse shook his head slowly.

"No. I have to believe Dad had good reason for his suspicions, so I have to co-operate. I owe it to him."

"Best we head for town come midnight," advised Duff. "Time we get there, things'll be real quiet. Count on McGinty. I'll go talk to him rightaway."

"Bueno," Stretch said placidly. "So, for now, we got nothin' more to jaw about."

Somehow, Jesse managed to subdue his apprehensions over supper that evening. His wife talked happily of her tour of Lone Star's vast acreage, the wooded areas, the rippling streams, the great herds viewed from a safe distance with Vern her attentive and entertaining guide. The atmosphere was congenial all during the meal; no caustic comment from Elva or her husband could have dampened the mood. As for the Texans, they appeared as relaxed as if they'd been part of this supper group for the past ten years. The Sherwoods resented their ability to make themselves at home; Jesse, his wife and brother didn't.

Neither Larry nor his partner lingered when the meal ended. They retired to their adobe to catch some sleep before it came time for them to accompany their co-conspirators to town. Vern read a while before turning in; the others called it a day soon afterward.

At 11.45 p.m., Jesse slowly eased himself out of bed and shed his nightshirt. While dressing, he gave thanks his wife was not a light sleeper. Dear gentle Trudy. Never in her wildest dreams would she guess her conservative husband was involving himself in a scheme so outlandish. Well, if there were no slip-ups, he and the others should be home before breakfast. And, in the event Trudy woke before his return, the note he had written earlier and now placed on the dressing table would reassure her. 'Back soon,' it read. 'Had to rise early to take care of a little business.'

Ready to leave, he donned a jacket

over his range clothes, tugged on his Stetson and quit the room quietly. He made no noise descending the stairs and letting himself out, and was not surprised to sight the four men sitting their horses a short distance south of the front yard, one of them holding the rein of a saddled skewbald.

He hurried to them and got mounted. No exchange of greetings, no conversation till they were far clear of the ranch headquarters and approaching the trail that would take them to the county seat.

Fred McGinty, a squatly built, button-nosed man of an age with the trouble-shooters, let it be known, "I'm doin' this for Mister Gelbart on account of he gave me a break. Just so everybody savvies — when it's done — I'm back to ridin' herd. No more picklockin' for me."

"You been cuttin' bits of wire all afternoon, McGinty," recalled Duff. "Got everything you need?"

"I know my business," mumbled

McGinty. "What *used* to be my business."

It was all of two hours after midnight when, entering Hart City, they slowed their mounts to a walk and made for a side street in the region to the rear of the impressive, double-storeyed City Hall. Spurs were unfastened and attached to saddles. They then walked carefully out of the street and to the rear of the building and, at once, McGinty went to work on the lock of its back door.

The deputy working the midnight to dawn patrol materialized, shotgun and all, just as McGinty nudged the door open. He challenged, but quietly.

"What's happenin' here?"

Without turning his head, Larry asked Duff, "Which deputy?"

"I'd know that voice anywhere, anytime," muttered Duff. "Jay Elhurst."

"And I know you gents," said Elhurst. "Includin' you tall jaspers."

"I'll keep this short," Larry told him. "We're here to grab the county

186

treasurer's records, do some checkin' and figure out how the mayor and his buddies're hijackin' tax money."

"The word is embezzlement," offered Jesse.

"Sounds reasonable," Elhurst said agreeably. "Go ahead. I'll be your lookout. Ain't likely a snooper'd come nosin' around at this hour but, just in case . . ."

In the past, Duff had visited City Hall with his boss. He knew the layout, so was able to guide his companions to the stairs and up to the administration offices. From a pocket, he produced a stub of candle. Stretch scratched a match to life and held the flame to the wick. They grouped before the door inscribed 'O. H. Kimmer, County Treasurer.'

McGinty tried turning the doorknob, shrugged and got to work with another of his improvised tools. He had the door unlocked and open in less than two minutes.

"I go in first," Larry insisted. "'Case

the window shade's up." He moved into pitch darkness. The shade had to be down, so he called the others in and advanced to the big safe. "What d'you say, McGinty?"

"A Dutton and Guyler," McGinty observed. "English make."

He began fiddling with lengths of wire.

"I suppose," sighed Jesse, "we should be thankful it doesn't have a combination lock."

"Wouldn't make no difference to me," said McGinty. "But, mind now, I ain't braggin' and I want to make it clear I'm no thief no more."

"You're honest, we believe you, just pick the doggone lock," urged Larry.

McGinty inserted bent wire and used it expertly for three and a half minutes. When he turned the handle and pulled the heavy door open, Duff positioned the candle close. They peered at the laden shelves. McGinty swallowed a lump in his throat and said shakily, "Just as well I'm a reformed character!"

"Holy Hannah," breathed Stretch. "Will you look at all that wampum!"

"I see more dinero than anything else," frowned Larry.

"I wonder which bank holds county funds," muttered Jesse. "Surely that's where this cash should be. There's so *much* of it."

"We'll think about that later," said Larry, dropping to his knees. The only ledgers he could see, two of them, were to the rear of the safe's floor. He drew them out and passed them to Jesse, "This what we need?"

Duff moved the candle again. Jesse delved briefly through both books and loosed an oath.

"*Exactly* what we need!"

"McGinty," said Larry. "Can you lock that door as easy as you opened it?"

"And this office door and the back door," replied McGinty. "It's important to be tidy. You leave doors open after you pick locks, you, might's well run an ad in the damn newspaper."

"So do it," ordered Larry.

A short time later, they were emerging from the rear door. The hefty lawman enquired, while McGinty relocked it in his own special way, "Get what you want?"

"And then some," grinned Stretch.

Jesse was hugging the ledgers to his chest and nodding vehemently.

"Fine," Elhurst said genially. "Don't reckon I'll be asked but, if some big shot gets riled up, I don't know a doggone thing. See you later."

They returned to the side street and their horses A little while later, with the town well to their rear, Jesse's impatience got the better of him.

"The hell with it," he growled. "I can't wait till I'm back at the ranch. Stand of timber over there to our right. We can make a fire if we can find a clearing. That'll give me ample light."

"We got what we come for boy," soothed Duff. "You got all the time you . . . "

"Duff, if you think Jesse's curious, take a look at Larry," drawled Stretch. "My ol' buddy's so blame impatient, he's apt to bust a gut."

"C'mon, what're we waitin' for?" scowled Larry, and turned his sorrel off the trail.

They rode to the copse and, in Indian file, moved through it to a clearing just wide enough to accommodate men and horses. Dismounting, Stretch began gathering wood. McGinty took charge of the horses and Jesse clung to those ledgers as though they were part of a raft and he in danger of drowning.

The Texans made short work of rustling up a fire, then hunkered with Duff and watched Jesse squat in its glow and begin turning pages. He was silent for some little time, both books open, studying, comparing, rechecking. Larry was wondering how long he could suppress his own curiosity when Ed Gelbart's second-born cursed bitterly and spoke again.

"A typical bookkeeper's mentality," he said. "All entries — in both ledgers — bear his initials."

"Otto Kimmer," said Duff.

"He's their willing accomplice, a rogue, but still thinking as a bookkeeper," Jesse said scathingly. "The compulsion to record everything. One of these ledgers is available for audit. As an accountant, I can assure you no auditor would detect any discrepancies. The other ledger is the one that damns them as embezzlers, the mayor, Kimmer, Orban and Markey, the sheriff and the other deputy, Neville. It's a record of monthly sums withheld from revenue exacted as property tax. County funds are banked in a special account at the First National — *minus* the generous amounts they keep for themselves. Apley and Neville are paid the regular salary of sheriffs and deputies, plus hundreds extra."

"Same with the other grabbers, them old Ed never trusted," muttered Larry.

"Damn them all!" raged Jesse. "When

taxes are raised, *they* benefit! Not the county, not the tax-payers, just Burford and his cronies!"

Larry's mind was turning over fast during Jesse's outburst, his denunciation of all but two members of the administration as embezzlers bleeding the county dry, his assurance that these records were all the evidence the county attorney could wish' for; he would insist on testifying for the prosecution and no defence lawyer in the entire country could bamboozle a Hart City jury into acquitting the corrupt councilmen and law officers.

"Yeah, fine." Larry rose and faked a yawn. "So now we head on back to Lone Star. Might's well catch some sleep before we tip off that Mirram feller, the only square-dealin' councilman and the only honest lawman this territory's got."

"I'll lock these in the ranch safe," decided Jesse, as Stretch kicked dirt onto the fire. "What time do you think we should . . . ?"

"After breakfast'll be early enough," shrugged Larry.

"You boys won't be goin' it alone," Duff assured them. "Maybe Burford and Kimmer'll be too shook up to turn ornery, but not Markey, not that fat hog Orban, and all the sharpers they've hired pack hoglegs and'll use 'em when it comes to a showdown. So fifteen, maybe a dozen and a half of our crew'll be right behind you. You'll need back-up, nothin' surer."

"We could arrive in force at ten or thereabouts," said Jesse.

"How long since you used a shootin' iron?" Stretch idly enquired.

"Don't worry on my account," Jesse said as they remounted. "If there's to be fighting, I'll do my share, but for Trudy's sake, I'll take no unnecessary risks." While they were quitting the timber to return to the trail, he remarked, "I'm sure Larry's already decided, and I heartily agree, we should keep the family and servants in ignorance. Trudy and Vern don't

194

need to know . . . "

"And your sassy sister'd get to speechifyin'," opined Duff. "As for that big shot husband of hers, well it don't matter what *he* thinks anyway."

"When you pick our back-ups, you'll do it quiet, right?" prodded Larry.

"Aim to choose them that's best with their guns," declared Duff. "And there'll be no blabbin'. It'll be done quiet."

Later, returning to the ranch headquarters, they went to pains to avoid rousing anybody. The Texans were last to lead their animals into the barn. They chose stalls for their animals and, while the other men offsaddled, fished out their makings to build cigarettes.

"Happy dream, amigos." Larry waved casually as Jesse, Duff and McGinty made to move out.

Jesse, hefting the appropriate ledgers, paused in the doorway.

"We all need our sleep," he pointed out. "You heroes are no exception."

"Sure," agreed Larry. "We'll be hittin' the hay soon's we finish our smokes and bed our horses."

It was dark in the barn after the other men left. Stretch was being patient again, also fatalistic. He waited a long moment before muttering, "Okay, you got somethin' on your mind. Nobody can hear us, so you don't have to hold out on me no more."

"Best we leave our critters saddled," Larry said softly. "We'll wait an hour. By then, they'll be sleepin' deep, Jesse and Duff But we'll have to sneak away slow." He gestured to the barn's rear door. "Get good and clear before we fill our saddles."

"We're gonna be back in town long before Jesse and the hired help rides in," nodded Stretch.

"Purty little thing, Trudy," remarked Larry. "Gettin' stronger, healthier every day. And too young to be a widow."

"Jesse's luck could run out, Duff's too," mused Stretch.

"It's right we should deal Elhurst

in," opined Larry. "Hell, he's entitled. But not Jesse. And Duff's no spring chicken."

"So we tip Elhurst," shrugged Stretch. "And take care of them sonsabitches our own way."

"We need the exercise anyway," Larry reasoned. "We've been livin' too rich here."

7

Beginning of the End

HIS shift ended, Deputy Jay Elhurst had eaten breakfast at an early opening cafe and returned to his home, but not to sleep. He called it home; it was just a three-room adobe at the north end of Hart City, a place to sleep, perform his ablutions and fix an occasional meal. There was a privy out back. The bare essentials were sufficient for the lawman locals regarded as just a regular deputy, a genial peace-keeper of carefree disposition, not exactly a deep thinker.

How little people really knew of him. Very soon after becoming a deputy here, his suspicions had taken hold. Of course, Apley and Neville were unaware of the contempt he felt for them. Thanks to his carefully maintained free and easy demeanor, they took him for granted. And that suited him because, as the late Ed Gelbart, that shrewd old observer, had surmised, Elhurst was biding his time. Without evidence of some kind, no corrupt administration could be challenged. Well, he hadn't waited in vain. Somebody had acquired evidence at last. He was grateful the somebody was a Gelbart, old Ed's elder boy. And even more grateful for the involvement of Messrs Valentine and Emerson.

Seated by a window offering a view of the town's northern approaches, he made a mental bet.

'You hot shots'll be back. Maybe with a couple dozen Lone Star waddies, but maybe not. Be just like you to want to go it alone, do it all your own way, just ride in and start raisin' hell. Sorry, boys. Not this time. I admire you plenty, but not this time. I'll be right there with you. We'll nail every bastard needs nailin', but we'll do it legal.'

In the early sunlight, he didn't need binoculars to spot and recognize the two riders far off, one straddling a sorrel, the other a pinto. He watched them veer off the trail to conceal themselves in a brush clump. Well, sure, he was thinking as he donned his hat. That made sense. No point their coming on in before the town opened for business.

Though he had worked the graveyard shift, he was too excited to be mentally weary, nor physically for that matter. He quit his abode and walked northward toward the brush.

Some time later, hunkered by their ground-reined horses, smoking, the Texans heard his foot-steps. Stretch jack-knifed to peer southward, hunkered again and said, "Elhurst."

"Fine," said Larry. "This way, we don't have to go look for him. And I want to do this right."

"Meanin' you parley with him 'fore we make our move," drawled Stretch.

"The old man'd want it done legal,"

opined Larry. "Well, passably legal."

They were grinding out the stubs of their cigarettes when Elhurst reached them and hunkered. He scorned greetings and declared, "I guessed right."

"You did, huh?" prodded Larry.

"Know your style, read many a bulletin about you hot shots," said Elhurst. "Them account books . . . "

"Dynamite," declared Stretch.

"Ain't forgettin' young Jesse's line of work," said Elhurst. "He checked 'em good?"

"So now we got proof," nodded Larry. "Two books, Jay, but only one for showin'. In the other one, Kimmer listed the skim-off, what they've been keepin' for themselves, Burford, Kimmer, the fat buzzard and another of his kind name of Markey."

"And your crooked boss and the other deputy," said Stretch.

"More'n more books in Kimmer's safe," muttered Larry. "Mucho dinero."

"And, when my partner says mucho,

he ain't whistlin' Dixie," said Stretch.

"Safe's stacked with the stuff," said Larry.

"The hog's share of county funds," Elhurst said bluntly.

"Jesse calls it embezzlement," offered Larry.

"That's what it is," agreed Elhurst. "And you couldn't wait, could you?"

"Look at it this way," urged Larry. "Duff Wheatley'll round up a bunch of Lone Star waddies — good with guns. Bet your butt Jesse'll come in with 'em."

"And . . . ?" challenged Elhurst.

"If them — artists at the Lucky Deal and the Chestnut act rash, there'll be a lot of lead flyin'," predicted Larry.

"That don't bother us none," Stretch assured the deputy.

"We'll take our chances just like always," said Larry. "But we'd feel real bad if Jesse stopped a slug. Or Duff."

"Or any of them good Lone Star boys," said Stretch.

"Right handy you spottin' us," remarked Larry. "We didn't plan on leavin' you out of it."

"Is zat so?" countered Elhurst. "Figured you could trust me?"

"Old Ed trusted you, and that's good enough for us," said Larry. "Left me a note, named the square dealers of Hart City — and all the sharpers."

"That old fox sure played his cards close to his chest," mused Elhurst. "All right, I better hear some names. We got to be sure. Even a wise old hombre like Ed Gelbart could make a mistake."

"You, Doc Richmond, Mirram, Trant and Doble the banker," offered Larry. "I guess — uh — county cash never was banked by Doble, even though he's a councilman."

"The account's at the First National." Elhurst showed his teeth. "Excludin' the money you saw in Kimmer's safe. And how many of them stinkin' thieves did Ed name?"

"Burford and Kimmer, the other

203

badge-toters, Orban and Markey," Larry told him.

"By Judas," breathed Elhurst. "He was onto 'em all."

"We ought to stop by City Hall first," decided Larry.

Elhurst fished out his watch and squinted at it.

"Won't be open yet. So we'll wait."

This morning, while the mayor was en route to his office at City Hall, Holly Orban emerged from his place of business and fell in beside him.

"Got some talking to do," the fat man mumbled. "Certainly, Holly, What's on your mind?"

"In your office."

"Just as you wish."

When Burford and Orban entered the building and climbed the stairs, the county treasurer was letting himself into his office. They traded greetings and Orban followed the mayor on to the larger office, there to plant his bulk in a chair and make his announcement.

"Gonna have to sell out and open another Lucky Deal elsewhere, Moss. Diego Wells maybe, Carneyburg, Flagstaff."

"You're quitting Hart City?" frowned Burford.

"The writing's on the wall," complained Orban. "Suddenly it's as if a typhoid warning was posted outside of my place."

"Business falling off?"

"Falling off? We're getting scarce any customers. No action at the games of chance — town-men aren't even drinking at the Lucky Deal. That's how it's been since the night that smart-ass Texan got wise to Clint Elphick."

"Your place was crowded that night," Burford supposed.

"That's the hell of it," scowled Orban. "The suckers're leery now. And I blame Valentine, not that those other do-gooders made it any easier for me, Doc Richmond, Mirram and young Gelbart."

"Pity it had to happen," said Burford.

205

"It did happen, and a place like mine can't operate without trade," said Orban. "A smart man knows when to quit. It's that time for me, Moss, so I'll take my cut of our nest-egg and move all my people to — I guess Flagstaff. I can wire Clint to join us there."

"Too bad you have to leave, Holly," said Burford, rising. "We have a good thing going here. But I understand your situation and, of course, our original arrangement will be honored. Any of us can pull out when he pleases and collect his share of . . . " he grinned smugly, "our secret fund."

That was how the scheme had worked. The bank accounts of the rogue councilmen, also Apley's and Neville's, contained no greater sums than would normally be saved by administrators, saloonkeepers or law officers; the rake-off cash was kept in the treasury safe.

Kimmer was smoking his first cigar of the day when they entered. He listened to Burford's instructions, got to his feet and nodded understandingly.

"You had to expect it," he remarked to the fat man. "All it takes is for a sore loser to prove one of your tablemen is pulling a fast shuffle. That'll do it every time. The smart money stays away and . . . "

"Don't rub it in, Kimmer," chided Orban. "Hell, you've always gotten on my nerves. You're a real pain in the ass."

"Just pay Holly off, Otto," instructed Burford. "Big bills, so they'll fit his pockets. It wouldn't look good if he were seen walking out of here carrying a cash box."

Kimmer produced his key, unlocked and opened the safe and, from long habit, dropped his gaze. Then he was loosing a gasp and flopping to his knees, rummaging.

"What the hell's the matter with you?" challenged Orban. "The cash is all there."

"The books aren't!" Kimmer fretted as he came upright.

Burford's scalp crawled.

"*What* . . . ?"

"They're gone!" cried Kimmer, trembling now. "I don't understand how — but they just aren't there!"

"Wait a minute!" Orban glowered at him, crimson with rage. "You unlocked that safe easy enough — and you're the only one carries the key!"

"The lock — must've been picked!" breathed Kimmer.

Burford moved closer.

"I don't believe you," he said grimly. "There'd be scratch-marks. I see no such marks." Of course he didn't; McGinty had been too careful, even working by candlelight. "Damn it, Otto, I want the truth"

"*I'll* tell you what the truth is!" snarled Orban. "He's stashed those account books and now he's holding out on us!" He advanced threateningly on the cowering Kimmer. "What were you planning? Blackmail, right? A fatter cut for yourself? Fix the books, make it look like you're a cleanskin and we're

208

the only ones taking tax money . . .?"

"That's crazy!" wailed Kimmer. "I'd never . . . !"

But the fat man was out of control, cursing obscenely, grasping at the first object within reach, the heavy brass ashtray from the desktop. He swung at Kimmer and the ugly sound of the blow chilled Burford's blood. Kimmer's face was suddenly a red mask. Burford made to restrain Orban, but not fast enough. Orban struck again as Kimmer sagged, then again; his skull was broken when he slumped to the floor.

"Lousy, doublecrossing . . . !" panted Orban.

"For pity's sake, shut up," muttered Burford. "Damn it, Holly, you always were too hotheaded for your own good."

Dropping the bloody ashtray, the fat man said sourly, "Chances are the bastard's been sneaking more than his share."

"That's not likely, but you punished him anyway," Burford bent to study the body. "Holly, you killed him!"

"Good riddance," growled Orban. "Listen, I'm not gonna hang for it. Come on now, Moss, we're in this together."

"As if things aren't already complicated," Burford said shakily. "What in blazes has happened to those *books?*"

"That's for *you* to worry about — *later*," retorted Orban. "First you have to . . . "

"All right, all right," Burford forced himself to think. "I'll cover for you, but now would be the worst time for you to be found with your pockets bulging. Better I pay you off later. I'll relock the safe, return the key to Otto's pocket. You leave now and — don't try to run. Just amble back to the Lucky Deal as though you haven't a care in the world. I'll wait ten or fifteen minutes before I raise the alarm. My story will be that I — just came into Otto's office and found him dead."

The fat man turned and walked out. Burford resecured the safe, slipped the key into a pocket of the dead man's vest — then began worrying about the missing books. It now occurred to him to check the closet and the desk drawers.

By the time he shoved the window up and thrust his head out to yell to passers-by, Elhurst and the trouble-shooters were entering Main Street.

"Fetch Sheriff Apley!" Burford called urgently. "The county treasurer has been murdered!"

Moments later, with City Hall in sight, Elhurst and his tall companions saw Apley and Neville hastily entering the building, closely followed by Joe Mirram.

"Well, well, well," frowned Elhurst.

"This ought to be interesting — so what're we waitin' for?" Larry growled as they began running.

They barged through the main entrance and took to the stairs just as the rogue lawmen and the newspaperman finished their ascent. Burford was talking when they appeared in the open doorway of the treasurer's office.

"Came in here a few moments ago — and this is how I found him . . ." The mayor broke off to frown at the Texans. "What are you . . . ?"

"Who's the stiff?" drawled Stretch, as they moved in.

"None of your business, so back off," ordered Apley. "I got a murder to investigate and I want no interference."

"It's Otto Kimmer," announced Mirram. "The county treasurer."

Glancing at the body, Larry assured everybody, "This loser got his sometime after — I'd reckon three o'clock this mornin'."

"And just how would *you* know that?" Neville demanded.

"Because he sure wasn't here when we left with the books from that safe," declared Larry. "The books that prove this town's got a thief for a mayor and two crooked badge-toters."

That declaration won mixed reactions. Burford and Apley traded shocked stares. Mirram tensed with his eyes popping. Neville swore with his hand flashing to his holster, then froze. Larry's Colt and both of his partner's were out, cocked and levelled before the rogue deputy's fingers touched his gunbutt.

"Jay," said Larry. "Draw their teeth."

Apley's jaw sagged as his grim-faced elder deputy disarmed him, then Neville. Elhurst also unhitched their manacles as well as his own.

"Hands behind your backs," he ordered.

"Great day in the morning!" mumbled Mirram.

"You can send for an undertaker after you've stashed these lowdown thieves in the county jail, Jay," said Larry. "And let's not forget one of 'em's a killer."

He cold-eyed Burford, who flinched and shook his head.

"I know nothing of . . . !" he began.

His protest was cut short by Larry's stinging blow, a backhander that sent him reeling.

"Valentine . . . " chided Elhurst.

But Larry uncocked and holstered his Colt, moved on Burford and grasped a fistful of the front of his clothing.

"The only honest lawman here wants to know why!" he scowled. "And so do I!"

"I swear I didn't . . . !" babbled Burford.

"You ought to wear them fine duds the mornin' you climb the gallows," Stretch calmly suggested. "Man might's well look his best when he hangs for murder."

"Valentine, what makes you so damn sure Burford's the killer?" frowned Elhurst.

"Heavy hunch, Jay," growled Larry, staring into Burford's dilated eyes. "I've heard it said thieves fall out — and *these* thieves steal *big*. That sale's packed tight with more dinero that you ever saw. So, if they got to wranglin' about it . . . "

"No mistake about the murder weapon," interrupted Mirram. "look at that ashtray — all bloody."

"Bet you can't wait to print *this* story, Joey," drawled Stretch. "Two stories, huh? The day this jasper stood trial. And the day he hung."

"Oh, hell . . . !" Burford sagged in Larry's grasp.

"Might's well get it off your chest," muttered Larry. "You're all through — and you know it."

"I didn't kill Otto!" groaned Burford.

"My ass you didn't," sneered Larry.

"It was Holly!" cried Burford. "Holly Orban! The damn fool turned crazy when Otto opened the safe and we saw the books were missing . . . !"

His voice choked off. Larry let go of him and asked Elhurst, "Good enough?"

"And then some," grinned Elhurst. "We all heard. And Joe and you boys'll make right fine witnesses." Stretch moved on Burford and spun him around. Elhurst used his own manacles to secure him, then crossed to the open window, muttering, "I don't

215

hanker to take no chances with Orban. He's apt to spook and try for a getaway if he . . ."

"Any way we can move this scum to the county jail without the whole town seein' us?" prodded Larry.

"I'm givin' it some thought," Elhurst replied from his position by the window.

Apley finally regained the power of speech; blustering was the best he could manage.

"This time you've gone too far," he warned the Texans.

"Hell, no," taunted Stretch. "We're only just gettin' started."

"We aim to collect every rotten apple in the Hart City barrel," declared Larry.

"You three polecats're the first," said Stretch. "After you're stashed in the hoosegow you'll soon have company — as lowdown as you."

"Will and me — we're officers of the law," protested Neville. "You got no proof we . . ."

"That's it — yeah — that's right," Apley said desperately. "You got no evidence."

"You sayin' you didn't know Kimmer kept it all in *two* books?" Larry was grimly amused. "Jesse Gelbart said it, so I guess it's true. Kimmer never stopped thinkin' like a book-keeper. He kept records of pay-offs, the dinero you skunks raked off of county taxes. No evidence? Like hell no evidence."

"We'll deny everything!" panted Apley.

"Lotsa luck," jibed Stretch.

"*Who* has this evidence — is it okay if I ask?" growled Mirram.

"The books're locked in the safe at Lone Star," said Larry. "Jesse checked 'em good. Stay cool, Joe. You'll see 'em soon enough, you, Doble the banker, the county attorney, every hombre that'll be most interested."

"How . . . ?" Mirram blinked incredulously, "How'd you — get hold of them?"

"How d'you think?" shrugged Stretch.

"Just busted in here two o'clock or thereabouts and took 'em."

"Holy Moses," sighed Mirram.

"Good old Ernie," Elhurst said from the window.

"Who?" asked Larry.

"I was hopin' he'd come by around now," said Elhurst, grinning over his shoulder. "Drivin' his rig. Just what we need." He leaned out the window. "Hey, Ernie!"

The goatee-bearded driver of the hay wagon about to pass City Hall reined in his team and squinted upward.

"Who . . . ?" he began.

"Me — Jay Elhurst," called the deputy. "Got an extra delivery for you."

"Wagon's full-loaded," Ernie announced, as if Elhurst hadn't noticed.

"Bring it around back," ordered Elhurst.

"Why?" demanded Ernie.

"In the name of the law," said Elhurst.

The driver scratched his head.

"What kind of a reason's *that*?"

"*Do* it!" bawled Elhurst.

"Comin'," shrugged Ernie.

Turning from the window, Elhurst nodded to the drifters. "We'll take 'em down now. Stretch, you keep 'em covered. Even in irons, they're apt to try somethin' foolish. Larry, you go down first, open the rear door and keep your eyes peeled. Be handy if that back alley's empty when we load my prisoners into the hay.

"My pleasure," nodded Larry.

He moved out and made for the stairs. The haggard Burford and the now-jittery Apley and Neville followed, prodded by Stretch and the deputy. The group paused only once en route to the stairs; Stretch took grim pleasure in tearing badges from the rogue lawmen and passing them to Elhurst.

Down below, Larry hurried to the rear door and opened it. As he glanced out, the hay wagon rounded the corner to his left. He stared along the alley; the only pedestrians he could see were at least three blocks away. Somewhere behind him, he heard Elhurst's voice.

"How's it look out there?"

"Clear enough," Larry replied.

The perplexed Ernie stalled his team close to the doorway and became even more perplexed when Apley was shoved out by Stretch, then seized by Larry.

"By dad!" he exclaimed, as Larry heaved Apley upward to disappear into the hay. "That's the sheriff!"

"You got good eyes, old timer," said Larry.

Together, he and Stretch lifted and tossed the rogue deputy, who cursed in the moment before he too disappeared into the hay.

"By dad!" Ernie couldn't believe his eyes. "That's Deputy Neville!"

Elhurst brought Burford out. He was accorded the same treatment by the Texans, swept off his feet and thrown into the hay.

"By dad!" gasped Ernie. "That's Mayor Burford!"

"You got to admit," Elhurst remarked

220

to the tall men. "Ernie's a mighty useful feller."

"Yup," agreed. Stretch. "He makes sure you know who you're arrestin'."

"Ernie, turn this rig and roll south," Elhurst ordered as he climbed up beside the driver. "When we make Murdy Street, swing left, cross Main and follow east Murdy to the back of the county jail. And, till I tell you otherwise, you forget who's back there in the hay, savvy?"

As he began obeying, Ernie complained, "I swear I dunno what's happenin' to this old town."

"*We* know," said Elhurst, trading grins with Larry. "And that's what matters."

The Texans walked along beside the hay wagon, keeping pace as Ernie drove down to Murdy Street, made the turn into it and kept going. They crossed the main thoroughfare and, soon afterward, the vehicle was stalled in the east back alley directly behind the county jail.

The deputy descended, fishing out

his keys, muttering further instructions to the mystified driver. Ernie was to deliver his load to whoever was waiting for it and guard his tongue, tell nobody of what he had seen.

While he unlocked and opened the rear jailhouse door, Larry and Stretch vaulted the tailgate, extracted the captives one by one and passed them down to Elhurst. Ernie was ordered to drive on, after which it was Elhurst's pleasure to install the prisoners in cells with willing assistance from the Texans.

They moved through to the office. Elhurst pointed to chairs, made a statement as the tall men seated themselves and voiced it as sternly as he could manage.

"I have to go see an undertaker now. He'll collect Kimmer's body on the quiet and get word to Doc Richmond to do — whatever he has to do — sign a death certificate and such. I'd sure appreciate you boys waitin' for me here, don't know if it'd be right for

222

you to go brace Orban." He moved to the street door and frowned back at them. "You'll be waitin' for me here?"

They were seated and giving him blank looks. He shrugged helplessly and left.

Larry made to build a cigarette, changed his mind and restored his Bull Durham to a pocket. Stretch eyed him sidelong and said, "Well . . ."

"Uh huh," grunted Larry.

"Must be near five minutes since we helped lock up them thievin' skunks," Stretch calculated.

"About that long," nodded Larry. "And there's more of 'em."

"Might be quite a time before Jay gets back," suggested Stretch.

"Might be," agreed Larry.

"And you never did like just hangin' around," remarked Stretch, "Just doin' nothin'."

"You don't like it either," said Larry.

"So?" prodded Stretch.

"So," said Larry, getting to his feet.

"Let's take a walk."

At about the time Jay Elhurst had sighted the Texans approaching Hart City from the north, Duff Wheatley, fully dressed and with his Colt strapped on, had wandered into the chuck-boss's adobe and helped himself to a cup of coffee. After that he was slightly uneasy and felt compelled to check on two fellow-Texans.

Finding their quarters empty, he became just a tad irritable and began rousing the hired hands of his choice, ordering them to saddle horses. He then commandeered the weapon of one who would not be accompanying him to town and went to the ranch-house.

The younger Bedoya girl was ordered to summon Jesse. "Without wakin' the little señora, if you can help it, Juanita honey."

Jesse joined him on the front porch a few minutes later, rigged in his range clothes and waxing curious.

"What is it, Duff?"

"What it is," muttered Duff, "is

224

them trouble-shooters ain't here."

"You mean . . . ?" frowned Jesse.

"Vamoosed," grouched Duff. "I should've guessed. Ain't this their style? Couldn't wait. Comes near time for a showdown, ain't nothin' can hold 'em. Hell's sakes, they could be there already, likely clobberin' that thief Burford or wreckin' the Lucky Deal — likely the Chestnut too," He offered the holstered .45. "If we left without you, you'd only follow us. Mind what I'm tellin' you now, son. If you're gonna be with us . . . "

"I can't stay out of it," growled Jesse, taking the weapon. As he strapped it on, he pointed out, "Everything has to be explained to the councilmen Dad trusted, and I'm the one who can make them understand."

"You stay back of us, hear?" warned Duff. "It'd break my heart to fetch you home over a horse, shot fulla holes. Your little lady wouldn't much appreciate . . . "

"May I also borrow a pistol?" This

225

request was voiced by Vern, emerging in his shirtsleeves to join them. "Pardon me for eavesdropping, Duff, but you and Jesse deliver your lines so clearly I couldn't help overhearing.

"Vern . . . " began Jesse.

"If whatever crisis is looming affects Lone Star, let's not forget I'm a Gelbart," Vern said calmly. "Whatever I need to know, you can explain to me while we're riding to town."

"Aw, shoot," sighed Duff.

At Jesse's instructions, Juanita waited for Trudy to wake before informing her he was headed for the county seat on urgent business and expected to return for lunch, or maybe a little later. By then, twenty-one men of Lone Star were riding fast toward Hart City, eighteen top hands led by Duff and the Gelbart brothers.

Walking northward along the alley running parallel with Main Street on its east side, the tall men did notice dust, but a long way off, only just becoming visible on the horizon.

"How're we gonna handle this?" asked Stretch.

"Like we always do," shrugged Larry.

"Rough." Stretch nodded resignedly.

"Best we move in from the rear," decided Larry. "Any females around, we got to do right by 'em, give 'em time to get out of there."

"I guess Jay's trick worked good," said Stretch. "I don't hear nobody runnin', so the fat jasper and his hired help just don't know."

"I aim to tell 'em anyway," said Larry. "Figured you would," drawled Stretch. "So . . ."

"Yeah," nodded Larry.

". . . so here we go again," finished Stretch.

Joe Mirram had returned to his office with his nerves jumping but his mouth tight-closed. The scene he had witnessed in the county treasurer's office had stirred all his professional instincts and given him hope. Big turnaround imminent, he assured himself, watching the street from the doorway. By now, three corrupt officials were behind bars, the mayor, the sheriff and the deputy who had so relished his added duty as tax collector. Nobody loves a tax collector; Mirram was no exception. Burford had named Holly Orban as Kimmer's killer, so now it was only a matter of time; he anticipated it would all be over in an hour.

'Those records,' he reflected. 'Hell's bells. With *that* kind of evidence — proof of embezzlement — no jury *anywhere* would acquit them!'

The trouble-shooters reached the rear door of the Lucky Deal Saloon. Larry tried the knob. It turned easily, because a barkeep had unlocked it a little while after sunrise. With Stretch, he entered a stockroom and crossed it to an inner door. It too was unlocked, and opened into the bar-room.

They arrived unhurriedly, moving past the bar, coming to a halt when all parties present were clearly visible to them, the two bartenders frowning at them, the fat man sharing a table with his yawning hired girls — not looking their best this early in the day. Orban eyed them maliciously, as did the tablemen with whom they'd tangled their first night in town.

"Just what the hell do you want?" challenged Orban.

"Well," said Larry. "We sure ain't lookin' for a shootout but, 'case some fool pulls a gun ... " He touched his hatbrim to the women, "you ladies ought to mosey on out of here, get some fresh air."

The saloon girls needed no urging; feminine intuition moved them to make their exit, not up the staircase but straight to the batwings and out of the building.

"My partner'll answer your question now — blubber-belly," announced Stretch.

"We're here for you," Larry told Orban. He heard a clatter of hooves, but didn't let the sound distract him, kept his eyes on the fat man. "Apley and Neville ain't wearin' tin stars no more. They're in the county jail, them and Burford, and we know you're the hothead butchered Kimmer."

"On account of," said Stretch, "Burford told us and Elhurst and Mirram."

"Burford's a damn liar!" cried Orban, lurching upright.

8

Free and Clear

THE barkeeps traded quick glances, crouched and dropped their hands under the bar. Orban's other hirelings sat tense, eyes fixed on the Texans.

"Burford cracked," Larry said coldly. "I guess it was the shock. Must've been a shock for you too, Orban. Them account books?"

"I don't know a damn thing about . . . !" began Orban.

"We got 'em," growled Larry.

"And they've been — what's the word, runt?" asked Stretch.

"Audited," said Larry. "Checked by Jesse Gelbart. So it's all over, fat man. Even if you weren't gonna hang for killin' Kimmer, it's for sure you'd melt off a lot of that blubber in a

231

territorial prison. You and the others — for hoardin' all that dinero, robbin' the taxpayers."

The hoofbeats were louder now. Some of Orban's men glanced toward the street and he made a fatal mistake, assumed the Texans too would be distracted and whisked a pistol from under his coat. Larry's Colt cleared leather at lightning speed and boomed and the fat man shuddered and began collapsing. The faro, blackjack and roulette dealers filled their hands and so did Stretch, just as the barkeeps straightened up, hefting and cocking shotguns grabbed from the shelf under the counter.

Larry sidestepped quickly. The bullet triggered by the faro man sped past his head as he returned fire. Simultaneously, Stretch's righthand Colt boomed and the roulette man wailed and reeled, his right shoulder bloody. The faro man, creased by Larry's bullet, was down and writhing.

Stretch lined his .45s on the bartenders

and was about to order them to uncock and drop the shotguns when the street window shattered. A couple of Lone Star waddies had hurled a sidewalk bench at it, and now they appeared there, they, Duff and the Gelbart brothers, all discharging sixguns. The back bar mirror was demolished, also much of the stock and glassware on the shelves. In shock, the barkeeps dropped the shotguns and raised their hands high; so did the unscathed members of the staff of the late Holly Orban.

Elhurst now barged in with gun drawn and enquired of the Texans, "You never heard of *patience*?"

"Can't wait to jaw with you, Jay," said Larry, cocking an ear. More hoofbeats. Some of the Lone Star men were headed downtown. "They makin' for Markey's place? Well, hell, the beanpole and me better get to the back alley again. Less Markey and his bunch're deaf, they've heard the shootin'. Now they'll hear them riders and . . . "

"And likely spook and skedaddle — the back way," growled Stretch, following his partner to the rear door. The tall men left Elhurst to take prisoners and ran south along the back alley, next destination the Chestnut Saloon — which a dozen cowhands with memories of hard-earned pay lost to cardsharps, loaded dice and a rigged roulette wheel were now reaching.

There was no holding them back, the cowhands who entered the bar-room of the Chestnut, all brandishing pistols, two of them still mounted. Well and truly intimidated, the few townmen who'd stopped by for an early drink made themselves scarce. The percentage girls loosed screams, startling a horse which promptly deposited a quantity of dung on the bar-room floor.

"Where's Markey and his sharpers?" the animal's rider demanded of the bartenders.

Both with their hands raised, both badly scared, the barkeeps shook their heads.

The Texans had figured it right. Markey and his crooked dealers were emerging from the saloon's back door, hats on and toting suitcases, when Larry challenged them from twenty yards away.

"That's as far as you run!"

Bags were hastily dropped and pistols drawn. Larry's Colt and both of his partner's boomed just as the would-be runaways opened fire. Markey howled, lost his grip of his gun and flopped on his backside with blood welling from a leg. His men triggered at the challengers, but wildly, inaccurately. One of them froze in shock as a slug from the taller Texan's lefthand Colt tore the top of his derby and whisked it from his head. Another went down with his gunarm bloody and the others frantically retreated into the saloon to face the wrath of the Lone Star waddies.

Outnumbered by irate cowhands checking marked decks, the mechanism of the overturned roulette table and loaded dice, Markey's sharpers threw down their pistols; to have opened fire on the invaders would have been suicidal.

The Texans reloaded and holstered their Colts and hauled Markey and the man with the arm wound to the county jail. The place was buzzing, Elhurst bellowing orders, Doc Richmond and another medico arriving to tend wounded prisoners, Mirram trying to question Duff and the Gelbart brothers and Dave Trant viewing the confused scene from the street doorway. He stood aside for the tall men, who hustled their prisoners in, aiming cheerful grins at the deputy.

"Looks like we've nailed the whole bunch," Stretch remarked.

"Room for two more," said Elhurst, glaring at the groaning Markey. "Just as well this jail was built so big. As for you tearaways . . . "

"We'd head for town around ten you said," Duff accused, but without rancor. "Never did mean to wait for us, did you? Had to be you started this hullabaloo."

"Damn it, Larry . . . " began Jesse.

"No use gettin' mad at us, amigo," shrugged Larry. "We figured Jay and us could handle it."

"Ain't that we don't appreciate you Lone Star hombres arrivin' when you did," Stretch assured them.

"Hell, no," Larry said warmly. "We were plumb glad to see you. It's just we kind of admire your little lady, Jesse. Be mighty sad if she got to be a widow."

"Didn't cross your minds I could take care of myself?" frowned Jesse.

"Just wanted to be sure, Jesse, that's all," said Stretch.

When all prisoners were secured, the doctors busy, hastily recruited locals keeping watch in the jailhouse and Markey, Apley and Neville snarling abuse at the shattered Burford, Abner Doble arrived. He had opened the bank on time and left his cashier in charge. And he didn't arrive alone; he was followed in by Gordon Crouse.

The banker was edgy.

"All I've heard — after that din of gunfire — are rumors," he complained. "Will somebody kindly explain . . . ?"

"We got 'em cooped, Mister Doble," declared Elhurst. "Talkin' about them stinkin' thieves."

"The mayor," said Jesse. "Apley and Neville, Markey and a lot of the double-dealers from the Chestnut and the Lucky Deal. The corrupt administrators, Mister Doble."

"Including Kimmer and Orban?" demanded Doble.

"Kimmer's dead," Elhurst said flatly.

"Murdered by Holly Orban," Mirram told the banker. "I was in the treasurer's office with Jay, our Texan friends and our corrupt lawmen when Burford told us." He chose his words with care, while Doble gaped at him. "It could be argued Burford was — well — encouraged to turn Orban in. A little psychology applied by Valentine. The man was already in shock and therefore vulnerable, but I doubt he'll retract his statement. So Orban will hang for killing Kimmer."

"No, he won't," countered Larry, now squatting on a desk. "He's as dead as Kimmer. When my partner and me braced the bunch at the Lucky Deal, Orban pulled a gun on me."

Doble mopped at his brow. He needed to be off his feet, so Stretch surrendered the chair he'd claimed. The banker sank into it, while Crouse lit a cigar and kept his ears cocked.

"They've always been so cunning, so cold-nerved," muttered Doble. "Burford was already in shock you say. And, to have murdered Kimmer and drawn a gun on Valentine, Orban must have been in a worse state than Burford, unable to control himself. *Why*"

"Well, sir," said Stretch. "I guess Jesse and Larry and me kind of shook 'em up."

"How?" asked Doble.

"We busted into City Hall last night," Larry coolly informed him.

"Jesse hankered to do what he calls an audit, so we grabbed the cashbooks."

"Otto Kimmer's safe," offered Duff.

"They're at Lone Star now, Mister Doble," said Jesse. "I've done a preliminary check and, though I'm sure of my findings — ready to testify in court — it would be appropriate for you to examine them also."

"*Two* ledgers, I presume," Doble said shakily.

"Good guess," smiled Jesse. "One available for audit and showing all funds, all tax money, properly accounted for, the other listed the amounts embezzled by your fellow councilmen, shared by Burford, Orban, and Markey and Kimmer, plus generous handouts to Apley and Neville. They were shrewd enough not to pay that extra cash into their bank accounts. It was hoarded, Mister Doble, packed tight into the treasury safe — a considerable sum, as you'd imagine."

"This is — pretty much what Dave Trant and I suspected," sighed Doble.

"We were in no position to bring any action against them, for the obvious reason. They'd have kept us in ignorance of that second ledger. We'd never have seen it, never have had proof it existed."

"Can you carry on now?" Jesse asked Jay. "Advise the county attorney, try to locate the circuit judge by wire?"

"I can carry on," nodded Elhurst. "Just as if I was sheriff."

"I predict you will be, and soon," said Mirram. "Matters have come to a head. Changes'll be made But I can't publish anything rightaway. I'll need all the details."

"Right, Joe," said Crouse. "The taxpayers hunger for positive information, not speculation."

Vern, who had enjoyed his participation in recent hectic events, came up with a suggestion for Duff.

"Why not have a rider return to Lone Star at once to alert Carmen there'll be two extra for lunch, Mister Doble and Mister Mirram? Inspection of the evidence should be postponed until all concerned parties have partaken of a good meal. Cooler heads must prevail."

"I accept the invitation," said Doble. "My cashier can take care of all business till I return, already proved himself capable when I was confined to my bed a few months ago. Joe, we'll use my surrey."

"Then you'll have room for me, if I'm included in the luncheon invitation?" asked Crouse.

"Dining facilities at our old home aren't exactly cramped," grinned Vern.

"So," said Duff, "I'll have one of the boys head on back rightaway."

He moved out and, as Crouse turned to follow him, the banker said, "My surrey will be waiting in front of the newspaper office."

"Thank you," said Crouse. "I won't keep you waiting. I just have to stop by the house and tell my wife not to wait lunch for me — and fetch a little something from my office."

Some ten minutes later, he was removing the 'little something' from his office safe, the envelope his late client had instructed him to open if and when Moss Burford ceased to be mayor of Hart City. Since Burford's indictment seemed a certainty, Crouse assured himself now was the time. He tore the flap and extracted two sheets on which, in his familiar hand, Ed Gelbart had set down his requirements. He read the document, then the note that began 'Dear Larry' — and laughed aloud.

Don't worry — you old fox. The document's simple wording will suffice. I'd have composed it in legal terminology, but it'll do, sir. It's legal enough.'

He replaced the papers in the envelope, pocketed it and left to walk to the *Journal* office. Moving along Main Street, he noted the many townfolk out and about, all of them curious. Hart City was in a state of excitement this morning, and small wonder; the sounds emanating from the town's biggest saloons suggested Lone Star hands were indulging in a wrecking spree.

Nobody appreciates high taxes.

Nobody appreciates games of chance rigged to ensure the house always wins.

The Lucky Deal and the Chestnut appeared much the worse for wear by the time the Lone Star men rode out. Abner Doble followed in his surrey, his passengers Joe Mirram and the lawyer. The column was headed by Duff and the Gelbart brothers and, typically, the trouble-shooters were content to bring up the rear.

They ambled out of town to the brush clump where they had left their horses, trading hunches.

"This'll set things to rights, huh runt?" suggested Stretch.

"I can't think of nothin' else needs fixin'," muttered Larry. "The grabbers — them that Jesse calls embezzlers — are stuck in the county jail. Don't seem likely they could weasel out of whatever charges they stand trial for, no matter how smart a lawyer they hire."

"I've been thinkin'," Stretch announced as they came in sight of their horses.

"Mighty useful habit," approved Larry. "Keep it up."

"Thinkin' about all the stealers, every kind of thief we've tangled with since way back when we started driftin'," frowned Stretch.

"We've sure known all kinds," reflected Larry.

They swung astride, hustled their mounts back to the trail and, from then on, let them choose their own pace, keeping the surrey and the column of horsemen well ahead of them.

Stretch elaborated on his ruminations.

"Rustlers, claim-jumpers, kidnappers, bandidos that hit banks and stage coaches and trains. A few crazies too. Loco gun-toters that kill just for the hell of it. All kinds of cheaters too, cardsharps, bunko men. I'm sayin' we've gone up against everybreed of two-legged skunk anybody could name."

"Ain't that the truth," Larry agreed.

"But big shots got to be the most lowdown of all," opined Stretch.

"Not all big shots're thieves," remarked Larry.

"Ain't talkin' about the honest ones," said Stretch. "Talkin' bout the buzzards that were runnin' Hart City."

"They're the worst," Larry said bitterly. "Honest citizens vote for 'em — and get suckered. Folks ought to be able to trust their lawmen and them they elect to work for 'em, their councilmen — administrators they're called. They pay their taxes and count on the boss-men for a square deal, and what happens? You get a crooked mayor, crooked aldermen and a crooked sheriff stealin' from their own treasury, stowin' dinero away for 'emselves, while honest workin' stiffs keep payin' high taxes."

"Lousy deal," grouched Stretch. "I guess it ain't no better in the big cities, huh?"

"Likely not," shrugged Larry. "But maybe, a hundred years from now, voters'll be smarter and there'll be no more thievin' buzzards runnin' things."

"Think that's how it's gonna be?" prodded Stretch.

"Amigo, I wish I could be sure," declared Larry.

Seeing her husband ride in with Vern and the hands, Trudy confided her relief to her sister-in-law.

"I'm so grateful they've all returned safely, Elva. I didn't really understand why they left in such a hurry, Jesse, Vern, so many ranch-hands, Larry and Stretch too."

"Must you refer to those ruffians by their given names?" sniffed Elva. "Such familiarity is downright unseemly. Mort also disapproves."

"As Jesse says, it seems to come naturally," smiled Trudy. "Because, rough though they are, they're so friendly, so polite to me."

With help from her daughters, Carmen Bedoya was more than capable of catering to three extra appetites. Over lunch, Jesse apprised his wife and the Sherwoods of the significance of recent nocturnal activity, the seizing of the county records and the violent aftermath, the Kimmer murder, Orban's death, the arrests that had left Hart County with only two councilmen and one law officer.

For once, Elva listened without interrupting, appalled by her brother's recklessness. Trudy, recovering from her initial shock, could only murmur, "You survived it all. I realize everything that happened was important for the local community, but your survival is, to me, more important than everything else."

"I suppose I have to concede you've achieved something," frowned Mort. "But, by Henry, I call it mighty high-handed, drastic action. I mean, breaking into the centre of administration, removing records from the county treasury . . ."

"This is the west, Mort," drawled Vern. "Pioneer folk can only endure so much. There'll always be some content to complain, voice their grievances in private and suffer under a corrupt administration. And, fortunately, there'll be others who'll resort to action — however outlandish."

"The word outlandish reminds me." Crouse set his fork down and delved into a pocket. "I'm sure Larry has forgiven your father for luring him to Hart County in such an outlandish way. Yes, outlandish is certainly the word though, as always, Ed Gelbart's whimsy was exceeded by his practicality. Larry, would this be your choice of the right time to reveal . . . ?"

"You mean the letter he left for me?" prodded Larry. "I'd as soon Jesse explained. He knows all about it. I told him, Vern and Duff too."

"Seems to me we deserve an explanation that makes sense," grouched Mort. "It was ridiculous — an estate this size willed to a — a . . ."

"Trouble-shooter, Mort," said Jesse. "One who combats evil in all its forms," grinned Vern.

"Dad did it deliberately," announced Jesse. "He knew it wouldn't stick, knew any challenge to the will would have to succeed. He did it just to bring Larry and Stretch here, because he respected their reputation and believed they'd achieve . . . " He paused to grin wryly. "Well, they've achieved it, haven't they? A corrupt administration has been wiped out — in no uncertain terms."

"Told you Gelbarts I don't want to boss this spread," said Larry. "And I meant it. So, now that Stretch and me have done what your pa wanted us to do, you can forget about challenging his will. You're welcome to Lone Star. All yours." He nodded to Crouse. "If sayin' it ain't enough, how about you write up some kind of paper tellin' how I don't want . . . "

"My client anticipated your decision," smiled Crouse, producing the envelope. "In his own hand, he prepared a statement by which you may relinquish all claim to your inheritance."

250

Elva and spouse could only gape. Larry accepted the document and the note and read the latter first, aloud.

"'Thanks, Larry. You too, Stretch. Knew you boys would get the job done' Well, I'll be a son of a . . . "

"He was really somethin'," Stretch said sentimentally.

Larry began reading from the other paper.

"I, Lawrence Valentine, hereby relinquish all rights to the bequest app — applicable to me — in the last will and testament of Edward Jesse Gelbart — and desire that — uh — said bequest be shared equally by his . . . " He looked at Elva and her brothers, then at Crouse again. "I sign this and . . . ?"

"And Mrs Sherwood and her brothers at once become owners of a third share of the estate," nodded the lawyer. "Which, I'm sure, was my client's original intention."

"Carmen!" Larry raised his voice while Doble and Mirram blinked at each other. "Fetch me somethin' to write with!"

The daughter and sons of Ed Gelbart watched Larry sign the document. Both Crouse and the banker signed as witnesses, after which Stretch grinned cheerily and said, "That does it, runt. We can ride on out soon as we want."

A short time later, while they were lingering over their coffee, Larry put a question to the brothers; neither Elva nor her husband could look him in the eye.

"What happens to this spread from now on is none of my business," he pointed out. "I don't own it no more, but I'm curious. What *will* happen to Lone Star now?"

"This is something I've discussed with Trudy at some length," said Jesse. "If Elva and Vern are agreeable, I want to stay on and manage the ranch with Duff's help. I'd be happy to resign my position with Cullen and Drew — by mail — and just stay on."

"I approve, Sis, and so should you,"

Vern said promptly. "There are several excellent reasons. Of the three of us, Jesse is the right person for the job."

"Another reason — the best of all — is Trudy's health," said Jesse. "This change, the climate here, have done wonders for her. From the time I began, courting her, she's never looked nor felt better."

"Mrs Gelbart," said Doble. "You'd be a welcome and attractive new member of the Hart County community."

"Now I'm blushing," murmured Trudy.

"We've always liked and admired Jesse," Mirram told her. "I'm sure we feel the same way about you."

"What do you say, Sis?" asked Vern.

"Say yes," urged Mort. "Come on, Elva, we can be on the next train out of here. Already I'm losing money. I have to contact my lawyers, call off the challenge to the will, pay their fees . . . "

"I agree of course," said Elva, still ignoring the Texans. "Then that's settled," said Jesse. "And now, Mister Doble, let's finish our coffee in Dad's office. I know you're eager to inspect the account books — especially the one you and Mister Trant were never meant to see."

"Eager is putting it mildly, my boy," said Doble. "By your leave, ladies. Coming, Joe?"

"Try and stop me," chuckled Mirram.

"Just before you go," Larry said, as the brothers got to their feet.

"Yes, Larry?" asked Jesse.

"Adios," said Larry.

"And lotsa luck," nodded Stretch.

"We'll be leavin' in a little while — quarter-hour at most," said Larry. "Done what your pa wanted, got no reason to hang around."

"Just like that?" frowned Jesse. "You'll accept no remuneration for all you've . . . ?"

"Got all the dinero we need, Jesse," drawled Stretch.

"I'm so sorry . . . " began Trudy.

"Thanks," Larry acknowledged.

"We'll miss you too, ma'am."

"And we're glad you're feelin' better'n when you got here," said Stretch.

"Thank you both," she said fervently, "I'll never forget you. Neither will Jesse nor Vern — nor Elva and Mort." She met her sister-in-law's challenging gaze. "You may not care to admit it, Elva, but *you* won't forget Larry or Stretch."

"No matter how hard you try, Sis," chuckled Vern.

"Don't call me Sis," she snapped.

Before conducting Mirram and the banker to the study, the Gelbart brothers warmly shook the Texans' hands and wished them well. "Safe riding, amigos," said Jesse. "And that comes from the heart."

"If you heroes ever weary of fighting other people's baffles and seek a career as actors, look me up in Chicago," Vern offered with a grin and a wink. "Other famous westerners have performed on stage. Colonel William Cody, for instance, Ned Buntline, Wild Bill Hickok . . ."

"And made jackasses of 'emselves," said Larry, returning his grin. "Who d'you think you're foolin'?"

By 3.30 p.m. of that day, the drifters had finished buying supplies in Hart City. Their horses were saddled and all gear secured. They were ready to turn their backs on this territory, but not before visiting the county cemetery.

Having located the last resting place of Ed Gelbart, they stood by it a while, Stetsons held to chests.

"He sure knew how to get what he wanted," mused Larry.

"Sure did," Stretch wistfully agreed. "Knew he'd be dead when we did what he wanted, but didn't never doubt we'd do it."

Studying the headstone, Larry muttered, "You're one sly Texan, Ed Gelbart."

"But we ain't complainin', Ed," said Stretch. "Right, runt?"

"Right," nodded Larry.

"No hard feelin's," said Stretch.

"No hard feelin's," said Larry.

As they turned away to walk to their waiting horses, Stretch cocked an ear and raised his eyes to the sky.

"Somethin' fazin' you?" demanded Larry.

"I guess not," shrugged Stretch.

"What d'you mean — you guess not?" challenged Larry.

"Just for a couple seconds there," sighed Stretch, "I could've swore I heard him laughin' at us."

"Your ears playin' tricks," said Larry.

"Sure," nodded Stretch.

"Where we are, there's no way we could hear him laugh," Larry declared when they were mounted and riding northwest out of town.

"No way," said Stretch. "But that don't mean he *ain't* laughin'."

"Damn right," grinned Larry. "Probably laughin' fit to bust."

Carefree, at least for the time being, the tall men left Hart County behind them.

They were again headed 'no place in particular'.

Epilogue

IN the evening of the day Joe Mirram's special edition was issued, with the entire community aware it had been rid of a corrupt administration, people crowded into City Hall for a special meeting.

Nominated by Dave Trant as caretaker mayor until the next election, Abner Doble proposed that Jay Elhurst be appointed sheriff and that two deputies of his choice be selected as his aides. Knowing Doble to be a man of his word, the people gratefully applauded his promise that, if elected mayor, he would immediately reduce taxes to the level maintained prior to the depredations of the Burford regime.

Later that year, being the only candidate, Doble became the new mayor. The manager of the First

National Bank was elected county treasurer and at once arranged transfer of embezzled cash from the treasury safe to the treasury account at his bank. The reduction in tax was made effective immediately. Trant retained his position on the council and, among the new aldermen was Jesse Gelbart, determined to follow in his father's footsteps.

Moss Burford, George Markey, Will Apley and Richard Neville, along with their hirelings, were sentenced to heavy prison terms.

Vernon Gelbart became one of Chicago's most popular and successful actor-producers and married an actress of whom his sister keenly disapproved. Despite Elva's spiteful predictions, however, the Gelbarts of Chicago were, in their private as well as their public lives, a devoted couple.

Gordon Crouse's wife presented him with an eight pound son. By mutual agreement, the boy was christened

Lawrence Woodville.

The children of Morton and Elva Sherwood became avid readers of dime western novels, to the consternation of their parents.

CALABOOSE EXPRESS
WHISKEY GULCH
THE ALIBI TRAIL
SIX GUILTY MEN
FORT DILLON
IN PURSUIT OF QUINCEY BUDD
HAMMER'S HORDE
TWO GENTLEMEN FROM TEXAS
HARRIGAN'S STAR
TURN THE KEY ON EMERSON
ROUGH ROUTE TO RODD COUNTY
SEVEN KILLERS EAST
DAKOTA DEATH-TRAP
GOLD, GUNS & THE GIRL
RUCKUS AT GILA WELLS
LEGEND OF COYOTE FORD
ONE HELL OF A SHOWDOWN
EMERSON'S HEX
SIX GUN WEDDING
THE GOLD MOVERS
WILD NIGHT IN WIDOW'S PEAK
THE TINHORN MURDER CASE
TERROR FOR SALE
HOSTAGE HUNTERS
WILD WIDOW OF WOLF CREEK
THE LAWMAN WORE BLACK

THE DUDE MUST DIE
WAIT FOR THE JUDGE
HOLD 'EM BACK!
WELLS FARGO DECOYS
WE RIDE FOR CIRCLE 6
THE CANNON MOUND GANG
5 BULLETS FOR JUDGE BLAKE

ARIZONA DRIFTERS
W. C. Tuttle

When drifting Dutton and Lonnie Steelman decide to become partners they find that they have a common enemy in the formidable Thurston brothers.

TOMBSTONE
Matt Braun

Wells Fargo paid Luke Starbuck to outgun the silver-thieving stagecoach gang at Tombstone. Before long Luke can see the only thing bearing fruit in this eldorado will be the gallows tree.

HIGH BORDER RIDERS
Lee Floren

Buckshot McKee and Tortilla Joe cut the trail of a border tough who was running Mexican beef into Texas. They stopped the smuggler in his tracks.

FIGHTING RAMROD
Charles N. Heckelmann

Most men would have cut their losses, but Frazer counted the bullets in his guns and said he'd soak the range in blood before he'd give up another inch of what was his.

LONE GUN
Eric Allen

Smoke Blackbird had been away too long. The Lequires had seized the Blackbird farm, forcing the Indians and settlers off, and no one seemed willing to fight! He had to fight alone.

THE THIRD RIDER
Barry Cord

Mel Rawlins wasn't going to let anything stand in his way. His father was murdered, his two brothers gone. Now Mel rode for vengeance.